AUGMENTED 7TH

AUGMENTED 7TH

The Journey of Last Hope

SAURABH GUPTA

PARTRIDGE
A Penguin Random House Company

To order additional copies of this book, contact
Partridge India
000 800 10062 62
orders.india@partridgepublishing.com

www.partridgepublishing.com/india

CONTENTS

For Pari

Thanks to

Suresh Prasad Gupta and Aarti Dayal (Dad and Mom) for always supporting and being with me,

Sumit Kumar (elder brother) for solving all my problems and being my mentor,

Sahil Kumar (younger brother) for listening to all my stories, and

Subhasish Mitra (friend) for being the first reader of my book and giving expert comments.

CHAPTER ONE

JONATHAN'S FIRST GIG

It was Jonathan's first gig in his college and he was pretty excited about it. He wanted to clean-shave before the show, but his bandmates told him that keeping a beard would give him a rough look. He was of average height with small spikes, black eyes, big ears, and a big forehead. He borrowed a famous band's T-shirt from one of his friends who didn't even know about the band. All he knew was the name of the band looked cool on his T-shirt. Jonathan didn't overreact on his friend's silliness because he was aware of posers from his school days.

It was a small gig organized by a few musicians of his college where only the college bands were participating since the funding was very low and they were not ready to bear the cost charged by bands out of the college for playing there.

Jonathan was the rhythm guitarist of his band, but he always wanted to play as a lead guitarist. It was not like he just wanted to, he was much better than the current lead guitarist. Whenever he got a chance, he always borrowed electric guitars from his friends who were having awesome guitars but didn't know playing anything else other than one or two scales. Even the band members of Jonathan knew that he was an awesome lead guitarist, but the current lead guitarist Joe used to dominate the band.

The gig was organized at the basement of a restaurant, which was very unfit for a gig. But with the funding being low and only few interested students in college, it was enough for them. The stage was just half a foot high from ground, and the controls of the sound system were set in front of the stage in the left-hand side of the main gate. There were not more than thirty to forty people in the gig.

'Are you nervous?' Frank, vocalist of the band, asked Jonathan.

'Ya, I am,' Jonathan said.

'Huh, the stage looks so dull, why can't they make a good stage?' Joe sneered, swinging his guitar in the air.

'Why don't you consider stage as your home and crowd as your family? Because even if the home is not well, good family members will make it look better,' Jonathan said, tuning his guitar that he borrowed from one of his friends.

'Look who is saying. The one who is afraid of being on the stage.' Joe chuckled.

'People are nervous before their performance only if they have set a level of expectation among their audience, and if not, they can be as calm as you are,' Jonathan murmured.

'What? What did you say?'

'Save your energy, guys, we are next,' Rex, drummer of the band, said.

Their band named Hangover The Banned or what they called HTB were second on the list because the popular bands were supposed to play last. If anyone wanted to know which band were leading the gig or which band were more popular in that particular area, they just needed to look at the running order of the gig. According to Rex, the popularity of a band was inversely proportional to the set list of the gig. The band before them was done. They were removing the cables from their guitars and were stepping out of the stage.

'Let's go,' Adam, bassist of the band, said, taking his guitar belt out of the box.

Rex sat on his seat and Frank was standing just in front of him. On the left-hand side of Frank, Adam and Jonathan were standing, and on the right-hand side, Joe was looking for cables. They were an alternative rock band and were going to cover four songs of famous alternative rock bands.

They started with the sound check and went on. They played all the songs quite well, although the sound was messed up. Even after their brilliant performance, only few of the senior band members came and appreciated them. They told them to work more on their sound.

Jonathan was excited about the photos and was eagerly waiting to upload them on a social media site and to show them to his friends. They waited at the venue till the last band's performance, although they didn't want to, but it was the brotherhood of musicians that was stopping them from leaving the place.

'I think we need to change our genre,' Jonathan said, moving out of the venue as the show was over.

'And like what?' Joe asked.

'Maybe thrash metal.'

'Are you sick?' Joe said.

'Why can't we? Frank has got powerful vocals; Rex and Adam have already covered many thrash metal songs. So what is stopping you?'

'There is nothing stopping me. I can also cover any song, but changing from an alternative rock band to thrash metal band will not be a good idea'.

'We aren't famous, we haven't set any base, we are on the introductory phase, and once we set a strong base for ourselves, we won't have to look back'.

'I think Jonathan is right, we can at least try it. There's no harm in trying,' Frank said.

'Then go and form another band. If you want to be in HTB, alternative rock will be the genre,' Joe snapped.

'It is not like that, Joe,' Rex said and Joe cut him off.

'I am done with this conversation,' Joe said and stepped into the taxi.

Jonathan went home with the pen drive full of photos and videos of his performance. He threw his shoes, switched on his lappy, and logged on to a social media site. He uploaded all the thirty-eight photos of their gig with the album titled as 'HTB, first live performance'. He didn't upload the video because it was of 485 MB and his net speed was very slow for it. Till night he got 132 likes on his DP and 70 on his album.

Next day in college was very impressive for Jonathan. All of his friends were pretty impressed with his photos, although they didn't know anything about music or were not there to support him, but still they were impressed.

'Hey, rock star,' Miley said, sitting next to Jonathan in the class.

'Aah, it's nothing like that.' Jonathan blushed.

'Here comes my rock star friend. I am proud of you, dude,' Dave said from the back.

'Thank you, Dave, but it's nothing like that. I am not a rock star. We just played our first gig. There is still a long way to go and become a good guitarist.'

'Hello, rock star. You burned the stage yesterday,' James said.

'You were there?' Jonathan asked.

'Naah. But I saw your pics.'

Jonathan knew that he has still a lot of work to do, and he always considered the fact that the quality of appraisal doesn't matter much, what matters is who is appraising you. He knew appraising on the basis of photos was just because they were his friends. He expected being appraised by a true musician who had actually seen his performance, like some of the senior band members. But he never got such an appraisal.

It was his second year and the semester breaks were just two months away. There was a four-day vacation from the next Sunday due to some sports meet and he was ready to go on a trip rather than joining the meet just for the sake of attendance. But due to the high budget of the trip and his concern about his savings for the new guitar, he cancelled the trip. This time he assured his band members that he will be having his own electric guitar on their return and was having a plan to convince his dad.

Many times he picked up the phone, dialed the number, and then cut off in the middle. He even started rehearsing and wrote the main points for convincing his dad to buy him a guitar. He used to make his friend sit in front of him as his dad and said all the things that he was going to say on the phone call.

One night he boosted himself and called his dad.

'Dad, I need to talk about something.'

'Yes, say.'

'Dad, look, I know that you are not very much excited about my music line, but one way or other, it is beneficial for my studies.'

'And how's that?' Jonathan's dad asked.

'Look, all the senior bands in my college get scholarship because of their band, all the band members get certificate which they can attach with their CV, they also get free attendance for any gig. Many facilities have been provided to them which others can only wish to have. And I have been also selected as a part of it. All I need is an electric guitar. If I will not return with an electric guitar, they will kick me out of the band,' Jonathan said in a very convincing way and just opposite to what the fact was.

His college didn't provide any facilities for the bands. Most of the band members were going through semester backs due to their attendance shortage due to their gigs outside the city. The college didn't even provide any jamming room for them. They considered these bands as a group of druggie.

'I can give you only 150 dollars, not more than that. But don't get too much involved in it.'

'Thank you, Dad,' Jonathan exclaimed and ran into the corridor shouting.

'Yeah, I am coming for you.'

With only 150 dollars, he purchased a cheap guitar and an amplifier. Taking it back to his room, he was not able to control the glee on his face. He unboxed his guitar, connected it to his amplifier, and played it for the whole night. He even missed his first lecture because of it.

CHAPTER TWO

THE FIRST BIG SHOW

He was eagerly waiting for jamming and playing with the whole band. But some of his band members, like Joe, didn't show up in the jamming room until a gig was just two or three days ahead. They were paying the rent of the jamming room, which was just a simple room, temporarily soundproofed by thermo cols and egg crate, by cutting off their monthly pocket money and it was only used for keeping the drums. They always used to fix the date of jamming, but somehow the jamming was cancelled by an excuse of any of the band members. The only guy who didn't make any excuse ever was Jonathan. He always used to reach on time and returned back by playing for hours with only one or two of the members. Playing with the proper band was becoming a dream for Jonathan.

'Is he coming or not?' Rex asked, opening the door of the jamming room.

It was a small room, one side of which was covered by a bed. They requested the landlord many times to remove the bed, but giving a room was enough for him. Near the bed, they had somehow adjusted the drums beside, which nobody was able to enter once the drummer was on his seat. The only facility that they got from the room was an attached washroom, although there was no supply of water in it, but it was still useful in emergency cases. The guitarists and the vocalist used to stand in one corner of the room, and the bassist Adam used to stand on the bed.

'I informed him in the morning,' Frank said, entering into the room.

'We should start setting our playlist because I heard that there is an opening ceremony for annual fest on the next Sunday and my friend is in the cultural department. So I can arrange our timing in that,' Dave said, plucking his amplifier into the socket.

'That will be great, our first show in college. Now my friends will have no any excuse to miss the show,' Rex said in excitement.

'Today we will cover a thrash metal song,' Jonathan said and everyone was shocked.

'Joe will never allow that,' Frank said.

'Okay, I am starting it,' Jonathan said, ignoring Frank.

Jonathan was having a processor borrowed from his friend. He took his lucky plectrum. He grabbed the power chord E and looked into the eyes of Rex, Frank, and Dave. They were ready. Power chord E, D, C#, C, and he went on. He was playing with his eyes looking at the guitar aggressively and it was looking like others were just following him. Suddenly Rex missed a bit and they stopped.

'Let's start again,' Jonathan said in way that he will complete the whole song, no matter how much time it would take.

As Frank sung the first line of that song, it looked like he was born for power vocals. It was looking like all the band members were born for thrash metal. It was not like that they didn't enjoy playing the alternative rock genre. They praised it like god, but there is always some genre in which one fits like a glove and this was it.

When they were at half of the song, suddenly Joe entered into the room with his guitar.

'Hey, hey, what is this going on?' Joe said, putting his guitar aside.

'This will be our first song in our playlist,' Jonathan said.

'Are you sick or something, we are an alternative rock band.'

'But now we are thrash metal.'

'I can't understand why you hate alternative rock so much.'

'I hate alternative rock? Are you mad? I praise alternative rock like god. Alternative rock legends are my inspiration.

But you are also aware that everyone doesn't fit in every genre. God has made a particular genre for everyone, and it's his duty to identify it in his life before the time passes out. Keep on trying out till you find the best place for yourself. You go in a restaurant and choose a dish from the menu because it suits best for you, it doesn't mean that the rest of the dishes are crap. Even if someone would say anything bad about alternative rock, I will be standing against him. It's not about being partial to any genre. It's just finding the right place for you,' Jonathan said and everyone was surprised. Even Joe was left speechless.

'Come and play, Joe,' Rex said and Joe plugged his guitar, glaring at Jonathan who was also glaring back at him.

They took two to three minutes for the sound set-up and they started. But just in the first riff, Joe missed the bit.

'Hey, don't stop, I will continue,' Joe said in frustration.

They tried it again and again, but were not even able to move to the second riff. Jonathan was looking at Joe's hand and he saw that he was struggling with economic picking. He was also struggling with triplet and all others technique, which were very much necessary for any good guitarist. Even while playing as an alternative rock band, he used to miss too many notes, but he didn't use to accept that. After the fifteenth try when everyone was miffed just because of Joe, finally Jonathan unplugged his guitar and said, 'Joe, you need more practice.'

'I need practice? Are you insane? The sound is messing up with me. There is no any fault in my playing,' Joe said with exasperation and started playing the first riff again while other members were just standing and looking at him.

'Jonathan is right, Joe. You need more practice,' Rex said, getting up from his chair.

'Shut your mouth and play your drums. I don't need lessons. I can play,' Joe squealed, trying the riff again and again.

'Joe, stop it. You are going insane,' Dave said.

'No, no. We will play alternative rock, no thrash metal,' Joe said, switching the socket off.

'Everybody here is on the thrash side,' Frank said.

'Okay. So this was your plan. Go to hell you all. I will form my own band which will not include posers like you. It will be a band of musicians, not wannabes,' Joe said, packing his guitar.

'Hey, stop. We are not saying you to leave. Just practice a little more,' Dave said, holding Joe's hand.

'Don't force me to be violent. And I will not wait for your orders. I am leaving the band and all of you will suffer,' Joe said, ramming the door and moving out of the jamming room.

Everyone else in the jamming room was looking at each other like 'Now what?'

Jonathan took a deep breath and sighed.

'The guitarist of Broken Sticks is available. They have disbanded and he is a very good old-school guitarist,' Rex said.

'I didn't want to end it like this,' Frank said glumly, sitting on the bed.

'Be professional, Frank. A band can't run on emotions and friendship,' Dave said.

'But brotherhood comes first in a band, after that, professionalism becomes an outcome of brotherhood itself,' Rex said.

'What Rex said is totally right, but we have no any options now. The show is on our head and we need to jam a lot. Rex, call the guitarist tomorrow and tell him the playlist. I hope he will fit in our band like glove,' Jonathan said.

'Hey, what's the playlist?' Dave asked.

'How much time we have?' Jonathan asked from Dave.

'I think thirty minutes.'

Jonathan showed them a list of four songs from major thrash metal bands.

'And this all we will do in two weeks?' Dave asked.

'I know that you all have covered these songs alone. Now we just need to make it one. Just like in the way a new song is made. Riff is composed, drum tracks, solo, bass, and when all things are put together, they sound like a call from hell,' Jonathan said, plucking his guitar back.

'Jonathan, sometimes you are too much philosophical,' Rex said, giving a four-beat start with his drumsticks.

Next day they were again in the jamming room, waiting for the new guitarist from Broken Sticks. His name was Wilson. He was having classes till five, so he was supposed to be late.

'He is just behind the building,' Rex said, ending his phone call.

'Do you think that he will fit?' Dave asked.

'We are totally dependent upon him. We have no any option, but I have heard that he is a very good guitarist.'

Suddenly a guy with long hair, Flying V guitar bag in one hand and a cigarette in another, entered into the lane.

'Here comes Wilson,' Rex said.

'So you guys covering thrash metal?' Wilson asked, shaking hand with the band members.

'Ya, I think Rex has already informed you about our playlist,' Jonathan said.

Saurabh Gupta

'I haven't covered two of them, but today we can play the other two. I will need some time to cover the other two,' Wilson said, entering into the room with Jonathan.

They all plugged in their instruments and started playing. The jamming session went well. Wilson looked very comfortable with other band members and was playing very tight. They played continuously for three hours and ended up with a deep feeling of relaxation. They moved out of the jamming room and entered a coffee shop.

'We need to change our name,' Frank said while taking a sip of coffee outside their jamming room.

'Point to be considered,' Wilson said.

'DragonSteel,' Dave suggested.

'That's impressive,' Jonathan said.

'So this is it?' Rex asked, twirling his drumsticks.

'I don't think that anybody has problem with this name,' Wilson said, and they all agreed upon this name.

They started jamming daily, and with Wilson in, their level of enthusiasm got boosted. The band was playing very tight and it looked like they were jamming from months.

The gig was on the next day and it was their last jamming before the gig. As Wilson said, he took his time and came with the other two songs covered very well.

'And be there tomorrow at sharp six o'clock. Because I can tolerate if you sleep with my girlfriend but not when you are late at a gig,' Jonathan said and everybody roared with laughter.

Jonathan wore his borrowed band's T-shirt with a blue jeans, black wristband, and hung bandana in his back pocket. He also used to wear rings in the ring and index finger, a steel watch, and a long necklace of inverted cross sign. He took his lucky pick given by his servant, his guitar, and moved on from his room to the college. As he entered into the college, he gasped in surprise. The crowd was huge. There must be more than five hundred people standing and cheering for the show. Jonathan was not expecting this much crowd.

'It is huge,' Wilson said, tapping Jonathan from back.

'Holy crap,' Frank said and gaped.

'This is gonna be too big,' Rex drawled, putting his sticks on the guitars.

'Even I was not aware that it would be this big,' Dave said, moving towards the backstage and looking at the mesmerizing view of the crowd.

'You will get ten minutes for the sound check and thirty-five minutes for the performance. Doesn't matter whether your set list is complete or not, after thirty-five minutes, we will cut the power off,' a guy mumbled, who was in a great hurry, with a hanging ID card on which something like 'Fest' was written in bold letters.

'Okay, okay,' Dave replied.

'What we are going to play in sound check?' Wilson asked.

'What we played yesterday,' Frank said and everyone looked at each other with a smiling face.

They were waiting in the backstage with guitars, processors, and drumstick in their hands when suddenly someone announced on the stage, 'And now we would like to call Dragon and Steel.'

'What the hell? *And*? There is no *and* in our band's name,' Wilson said, taking the water bottle and moving towards the stage.

'It was expected,' Jonathan said and all the band members moved onto the stage.

The crowd was looking much more gigantic from the stage. They were shouting, cheering, and were very alive.

'I am gonna die,' Dave said.

'I am having stage-o-phobia,' Rex said coldly while sweating.

'But I am feeling like home,' Frank drawled, putting the mic onto the stand.

'This is our time, guys. We will show them what thrash metal is,' Jonathan said, signaling the soundman to raise the guitar volume.

They started their sound check individually and it was looking very clear that the crowd was not enjoying it. The soundman was setting tone to its highest level on the bass guitar that Dave was arguing to keep down and the vocals of Frank was also looking very low in comparison to other instruments due to the low mic sound. It was clear that the soundman was not having any experience of handling metal bands. Some of the audience started hooting. Rex got nervous and started acting weird.

'Calm down, Rex, calm down. Once we all set up, we will blow them up,' Wislon said, holding Rex's hand when he was moving here and there in nervousness.

'Okay, okay,' Rex said, wiping sweat from his head.

They were still not satisfied with the sound and the time was passing by. Sound of Jonathan's guitar was too high, tone of Rex was still not lowered, mic on the snare was very low, and that on the bass drum was too high. Wilson for a second looked at the crowd.

'We need to start, otherwise we will miss our playlist,' Wilson said.

'But the sound,' Rex argued.

'We can't expect much from this sound system,' Wislon said and moved towards his position and all others also moved.

'Sorry for the delay, but with such a messed-up sound system, even the deaf would die,' Frank said in such an attitude that it caught everyone's attention. The crowd responded positively to the mind-boggling start of Frank.

'So our first song is all about ruling the world,' Frank said and they burned the stage. Their stage presence was awesome. Jonathan used to say that stage presence as a band is nothing more than enjoying your music, because if you will enjoy your music, others will as well.

Most of the audience were not aware of the song but were still enjoying because they were playing with such enthusiasm, were enjoying it a lot, and as the first song ended, the eardrums blew away due to the shouting, but suddenly a guy with an ID card around his neck came running in the middle of the stage and said to Frank, 'Now you have only ten minutes', but suddenly Wilson started the second song. It was all planned by them that they will start the next song without any announcement. The guy with an ID card around his neck ran back to the sound system signaling the time cut-off to Frank, and Frank was in shock. He looked behind and they were not aware about it and were playing in a way that they will end the set list. For a second Frank thought, took a deep breath, and started the song. Suddenly in between the song, Frank saw Joe standing into the crowd like a spy agent trying to see the show, but at the same time hiding himself. Frank smiled and the song ended well and the crowd's response was awesome.

'Guys and girls, we are very sorry but we will not be able to perform our next two songs due to the shortage of time. This is what we call mismanagement at its best. Thank you, people, we love you. Stay heavy, stay raw,' Frank said and pulled the mic out of the stand aggressively. Other members were like 'What has happened?' They were still not able to understand. Frank told them to move out of the stage.

'What happened?' Wilson asked.

'That guy came and said we have only ten minutes more, but till then you all had started the song.'

'It was planned,' Rex said.

'I know. Let that guy come, I need to settle something.'

On the same night, Frank messed up the scene by indulging into a fight with that management guy when he yelled at Frank to whatever he said. Frank got suspended for two weeks, and till the time vacations started, there was no jamming because their jamming room was snatched from them due to the increasing debt.

CHAPTER THREE

THE STORY OF RIFFSLAND

It was the last day of college before the start of the summer vacations. Till then, by saving money, Jonathan was able to buy a secondhand processor from his classmate Dino. Jonathan was totally involved into metal. His room was full with posters of metal bands. He always used to play for hours, covering a number of metal songs. He did what his dad said not to, getting too much involved into it.

He went home after the last class. He was having a full-proof plan to cover many songs, learning many techniques, reading biographies of music legends, watching documentaries. He deleted everything from his laptop and filled it with discographies of bands. He was having full live shows, live recordings. These two months according to Jonathan were very crucial for him for his skills and knowledge in metal.

Last time he visited home in the months of winter and it was long ago. He was the only child of his parents. He used to live in his home with his mom, dad, and their old servant whom Jonathan was very much attached to.

His name was Sivur. Sivur was there in the house before Jonathan was born. Jonathan used to spend more time with Sivur than his parents. But this was just because his mom and dad both were working. They loved Jonathan very much and Jonathan loved them back too. They cared for him more than anything else in the world, and they worked hard to make Jonathan's future bright. Last time when Jonathan visited home, Sivur was not there, he was at the farmhouse. But this time he was there.

Entering into the house in a hurry and by throwing his backpack, Jonathan shouted, 'Sivur, Sivur!'

'I am here, in the rest room.'

Jonathan entered into the room and saw Sivur cleaning the glasses. Jonathan ran towards Sivur and hugged him tightly. Sivur was an old man with white beard and very deep blue eyes. He always used to wear a baggy shirt tucked under a formal trouser with black leather belt. Jonathan hadn't seen Sivur in any other dress than that. Only the color of the dress used to change. He was very calm and polite, and his every word was a reflection of his politeness. Jonathan didn't know any relatives of Sivur other than his one friend named Borish who took care of Jonathan's father's farmhouse and an aged lady who used to visit twice or thrice in a year. Sivur used to say that the lady was his cousin. But Jonathan always doubted on that because neither her face nor her way of talking looked like a cousin. Sivur always talked with the lady with due respect. One of the most suspicious things about that lady was she always used to stare at Jonathan whenever she saw him in the house, and she always visited the house

33

when Jonathan was there. Jonathan always thought it as a mystery or just a coincidence.

'I am too old for this type of tight hug,' Sivur said, feeling uncomfortable.

'I have many things to tell you, Sivur, about my band, about my guitar, and many more. I missed you so much, Sivur,' Jonathan said, making Sivur sit on the table.

'Calm down, young boy. I am not going anywhere for the next three months and you are also here. This beard doesn't suit you, go and shave it,' Sivur said, touching Jonathan's beard.

'It gives me a rough look, Sivur, which is important for my band.'

'But your parents wouldn't like it. They will like the professional look on you.'

'Yeah, I know. I will, Sivur. But I need to tell you all the things first.'

'Go and get fresh. You have come from a long journey. We have the whole night to talk.'

'Jonathan, are you there?' Jonathan's mom Kate asked from the stairs.

'Yes, Mom,' Jonathan said and ran towards the door.

'Mom,' Jonathan said and hugged his mom.

Jonathan's mom had green eyes and her lips were very thin and pointed. She always used to wear earrings in her big ears, which were similar to Jonathan. She also used to tie her hair on the top and always used to wear a scarf.

'Oh my dear Jonathan. You have gone weak. I am going to visit the paying guest owner and complain about your food. By the way, your lunch is ready. I will be not coming up for the night. Daddy is out of the town. He will be back tomorrow. Forgive your parents for not being with you on the first night,' Kate said in a hurry, taking her umbrella out of the shelf.

'It's okay, Mom. You all are doing it for me. Love you, Mom.'

'Love you too, my son,' Kate said, closing the door and moving out.

Jonathan was mature enough to understand how busy a private professional life is, and he understood the feelings of his parents. He never complained about them being out of the house, because when they used to be home, they spent the most precious time together.

Jonathan moved upstairs to his room where he spent his childhood. He opened the door and the room was still the same, the small double-storey bed with a blue-colored quilt on it. One side of the room was occupied by a reading table, with a black table lamp, a pen holder, and a digital watch, which was not working. The walls of the room were full of poster of musicians, which was Jonathan's first preference. The walls also included the paper cutting of many interviews of famous musicians.

Jonathan moved towards the study table and opened the door, which opened into the backyard of his house that was full of used materials and garbage.

'I am not going to sleep in my room. I will sleep with you,' Jonathan said, sitting on the table on which Sivur was serving the food.

'You are now too old to sleep with me. Now you don't have nightmares,' Sivur said, putting the chicken bowl onto the table and taking out a plate for himself.

'No, I said I will sleep with you and it's final. And you promised me, Sivur,' Jonathan said, taking a bite of chicken.

'Okay, okay. Finish your dinner first. You are still a small child, Jonathan. You need to grow up. Time is not far when all the burden will be on you.'

'For that, I have lots of time. Give me your plate,' Jonathan said, picking up Sivur's plate and moving towards the kitchen.

It was a scary night. There was power cut due to heavy rain. Dreadful lightning was shaking the windows. The whole house, which was quite big for two people, was buried into darkness. Unaware of this, Jonathan was sleeping in his room when Sivur entered into the room with a candle in his hand.

'Jonathan. Wake up.'

Jonathan turned around and jumped on the bed with surprise.

'Oh my god.'

'I knew that when you will wake up, you will get scared and shout for me. So I came up to wake you up.'

'I was not sleeping. I was just lying down. I already said that I am going to sleep with you, and with such a paranormal condition, you can't leave me alone,' Jonathan mumbled, getting away from the window.

'Come with me.'

'Sivur, how can you live in this big house all alone? The monsters under your bed can devour you anytime,' Jonathan said, moving downstairs by holding Sivur, who was holding the candle into his hand.

'Big house? It's only a single-floor building with two rooms at the ground floor and two at the first floor, and at this age, even the monsters know that their attempts will be a failure.'

'But still. What if it would be a big monster?' Jonathan said, entering into Sivur's room, and Sivur put the candle on the table that wiped out the darkness only up to the level of visibility.

Sivur moved towards the couch and sat on it, taking a deep long breath.

'Hey, are you not sleeping?' Jonathan said, getting up from the bed.

'As a youngster, waking up is a difficult task, and as an old man, sleeping is a big challenge.'

Jonathan pushed another couch and placed it just beside Sivur's couch.

'Go to sleep. You need not stay awake with me,' Sivur said, lying back on his couch.

'I want to listen to the story of Riffsland,' Jonathan requested, moving out of his couch.

'Riffsland? You have been listening to this story right from your childhood. Don't you get bored?'

'Bored? I can keep listening to this story continuously for the whole day. Every time I listen to this story, it gives me goose bumps. Please, Sivur. Please,' Jonathan begged, and suddenly heavy sound of lightning shook the windows.

'I hate these freaky sounds,' Jonathan said, moving closer to Sivur.

'Zorich Plutos, Valdus Lehmington, and Rother Fredman were considered as the living underground legendary musicians of their time. But instead of their legendary music sense, their popularity was least, and they were the one who tried to hide their talent from becoming popular. Zorich Plutos was a lead guitarist, Valdus Lehmington was a bassist, and Rother Fredman was a vocalist. They didn't ever try to form a band. They were having some hidden objectives, which they were trying to achieve through their legendary music. Everyone around these three legends suggested them to form a band, and many record labels assured hiring them if they would come up with a proper band, but they didn't care. Some of them, who were close to these three, are still alive and only few of them have been able to see them playing. They say that they have never seen such musicians in their life. They also say that when Zorich and Valdus started playing their guitars, it looked like the nature has also paused itself to hear them playing. Each single note they played and riff they hit looked like the most powerful thing they have ever heard. And the vocalist Rother was like the guy from heaven whose voice was gifted by gods. His vocals were enough to shake the earth. One thing they always said about these three musicians was they were having some energy in their instruments and voice that was intangible but was very powerful. But one day they got vanished. There was not even a single clue about their instant went out. It was like getting vanished by some extraterrestrial bodies.

'Under the guidance of Valdus Lehmington, the bassist, the other two went with him to the jungles of Amazon. They entered into the jungles of Amazon through the city Manaus in Brazil. These three musicians went deep into the jungle. They went out of food, water, and other life-survival kits. But they were having a plan. After getting deeper and deeper into the jungles of Amazon, which looked untouched by humans, finally Valdus Lehmington found the place from where his dreams started taking shape. Valdus, at the place known as the Pinch Point, formed the hidden world of musicians known as Riffsland. By their unmatched talent in music, they developed the hidden source of energy of their music.

'After forming the world Riffsland, these three musicians divided their work to build this new city into an actual world of musicians. Valdus Lehmington engaged himself in making the rules for the city, Zorich Plutos became the recruiter of Riffsland and started visiting gigs, clubs, bars, wherever the bands performed to select the musicians to make them a citizen of Riffsland and develop their talent, while Rother Fredman started making musical instruments for Riffsland. Slowly and steadily this world of Riffsland became a city of thousands of talented musicians. With the enhancing skills of the citizens of Riffsland, the three legends decided to form level of their instrument according to their level of playing and skills. The first level was birth, then Dorian, then shredder, and finally, the legends. Citizens of Riffsland started forming bands among themselves. The instrument which they played used to evolve after each level of their skill. Births were the new ones who learnt music. Dorians were the one who were good musicians but were not able to turn their instruments into weapon. Shredders used to help The Three in their work and were able to transform their instruments into weapons, and finally, the legend was able to call the warriors who were intangible.'

'Hey, don't forget to explain who the warriors were. It's my favorite part,' Jonathan asked excitedly, interrupting Sivur in the middle of his story.

'Okay, okay. I don't know why you are so much crazy about this story. It was only in the hands of the legends. Each note of the instrument used to give birth to a warrior and a combination of these notes like a riff, solo, blast beat, and drum roll gave birth to a group of warriors. These warriors were only raised on the night of two festivals. These were the two biggest festivals in Riffsland. It was used only to show the power of music. These warriors raised by the legends were not tangible, but their power could be felt. Two main bands which were on the level of legends started enhancing their skill beyond their limits of control. These two bands were The Wargskult and The Guttadevers. But one night in a meeting of these two bands and The Three, The Guttadevers went into an argument with Wargskult, and the lead guitarist of Guttadevers raised a warrior and attacked the drummer of Wargskult with it. Everyone was stunned because before that, no one had used a warrior for attacking a living being. The three legends abandoned The Guttadevers from Riffsland and ordered them to move out of Riffsland on the next morning. But on the same night of the meeting, The Guttadevers raised an army, which wasn't done by anyone in Riffsland, and they attacked the city with the raised army. But Wargskult fought back by raising an army from their playing and battled with The Guttadevers. That night is known as the Darkest Night. People were being killed, slaughtered, and everybody was involved in the battle, some through their warriors and some by turning their instruments into weapons. The night was looking a never-ending battle.

Everyone was witnessing the next level of skills which is now known as the Prime Ones. Only the Guttadevers and Wargskult have been able to get onto that level from where they can call a whole army which can fight for them. Somehow on that night, Wargskult was able to push back The Guttadevers. But in that epic battle, they lost their lead guitarist Andrew Blake. It is said that when he was playing his last notes, his hands were bleeding and the whole guitar got colored with his blood and turned into a red guitar which is called as the Blood Shredder. Still no one knows that where The Guttadevers went. But it is sure that they didn't die and they are still there, planning for a return. After that night, the raising of army or warrior was abandoned and the band Wargskult disbanded because of the loss of their lead guitarist. With no other band on the level of a prime one, the protection of Riffsland has always been on edge. Now if The Guttadevers would attack the city without Wargskult, its protection will be not so easy. They looked upon for every possible guitarist for recruiting him in Wargskult, but till now no one has been able to get onto that level. Therefore the members of Wargskult hid their instruments in nature so that the bad one couldn't misuse it. It is said that their instruments are so much powerful that if the members of The Guttadevers would get it, it will become impossible to stop them.'

'Tell me about the members of Wargskult,' Jonathan asked.

'The vocalist of Wargskult, Stepehen Marflet, lives in the southern region of Riffsland known as the Last Fret. It is said that the Last Fret is always covered with snow and winter never leaves the place. He lives there for

protecting his mic, which has not been used after the war with Guttadevers. The mic is known as The Pitch of Soul, which has been buried deep inside the snow. He lives there with other vocalists of Riffsland who crosses the level of Dorian and attains shredder. The drummer of Wargskult, Blake Dyer, lives in the northern region known as the Mythius. And it is said that for protecting his drums, which is called as the Torpido, he has hid the drums inside one of the trees from billions in Mythius. The rhythm guitarist, Luke Knight, who is married to Sarah Knight, the greatest flute player of all time, live together in the western side known as The High Hills for protecting his guitar, which is called as Floating Wave, which has been hid inside the mountains. The bassist—'
'Finn Henwood, who is married to Daniela Henwood, the greatest flamenco player,' Jonathan interrupted Sivur.

'Yes, and they both live in the eastern side known as the Rosewood. And his bass is being protected by the sea. His bass guitar is called as The Geblur. And the last one was the lead guitarist of Wargskult, Andrew Blake, who was married to Isabel Blake, the violin player. His guitar, called as The Blood Shredder, is kept in the middle of Riffsland, which is protected by The Three. It is said that the place where his guitar has been kept is only known to The Three and the other legends and no one has ever been able to even get near to that guitar because of uncontrollable power, which was only controlled by Andrew Blake.'

The night was very blood-curdling, but with Sivur around him and by thinking about the city of Riffsland, Jonathan was able to sleep on that night.

CHAPTER FOUR

TRIP TO FARMHOUSE

The vacations were not going in the way Jonathan had expected. Just after two days of his arrival, he was ordered to go to the farmhouse. The farmhouse was handled by one of Sivur's friends named Borish whom he didn't like much. But as it was an order from his parents, he was bound to follow. He knew that his uncle will keep him engaged in boring farmhouse works, and after his return, he will be so much exhausted that only bed will be the thing of prime importance. And the worst part of it was he was not allowed to take his guitar and amp to the farmhouse.

'Why can't you come with me, and what does my guitar has to do with this farmhouse?' Jonathan asked, packing his bag.

'I have to take care of this house, and about your guitar, ask your dad,' Sivur said softly, folding Jonathan's shirt.

'I heard that you have suggested this farmhouse idea,' Jonathan asked suspiciously.

'I am not sure about it.'

'I don't like this farmhouse.'

'This farmhouse belongs to your family and you must go and learn the know-how of your farmhouse.'

'Are you ready, Jonathan?' Jonathan's dad asked.

'Yes, Daddy,' Jonathan replied coldly, closing his backpack.

His dad was a tall guy named Williams Bradman with a thin mustache and a 24/7 serious look, which Jonathan didn't like much. He always talked about abdicates, manners, and always tried to make Jonathan a professional charming boy from his childhood. Although he was very soft-hearted, he didn't want to let other people know about it.

'Be there at the main gate in five minutes, I am taking the car out,' Jonathan's dad said, moving out of the gate.

'Okay.'

'Enjoy your holiday, son,' Sivur said.

'I will miss you, Sivur,' Jonathan said and hugged Sivur tightly.

'Where are you, my son? We are getting late,' Williams shouted from outside the house with the sound of horn.

'Coming, Dad,' Jonathan said and started moving towards the main gate by looking at Sivur who was waving goodbye with a smiling face.

'Dad, why can't I take my instruments to the farmhouse' Jonathan asked, putting on the seat belt.

'Son, I have never stopped you from doing what you want, but you know Uncle Borish is very much peace-loving and doesn't enjoy loud music. I don't want to create trouble for him as he has already done many things for our family without having any blood relation with us. He is just a friend of Sivur but closest to our family.'

'I know, Dad. But I don't like him much because he makes me work for the whole day and talks about politics at the dinner table.'

'He is like that from the start and no one can change him.'

The small board covered in dirt and mud with the heading 'Brikeny Bar' was a sign that the farmhouse was just half a kilometer ahead. It was getting close to the time of sunset, and at that time, the view of the farmhouse from the streets looked mesmerizing. The gate of the farmhouse was big and new. The farmhouse was an isolated but big place. From the farmhouse, one could only see the only single road with scattered greenery on both sides.

'Here we come,' Williams said.

'They have changed the gate,' Jonathan said coldly.

'Yes, and it looks much better than the previous one.'

'Oh oh, here you come, my little Jonathan,' Uncle Borish said as he saw Jonathan stepping out of the car.

He was a short-heighted man with a cowboy hat on top and brown leather boots. He always used to have a toothpick on the side of his lips.

'Hello, Uncle Borish,' Jonathan said with a fake smile, taking his luggage out of the car.

'How are you, Borish?' Williams asked, locking the car.

'It's been long, Mr. Bradman, nice to see you,' Uncle Borish said, shaking hands with Jonathan's father in an expected formal way.

It was dawn till then. When Jonathan was a kid, the nights of the farmhouse used to be very haunting for him, especially when he was told to go and have a look at the sheep.

'So you are going to spend the next three months here?' Uncle Borish asked Jonathan, stepping towards the house with William. 'Yes, I also heard that.'

'Don't worry. Farmhouse is now not so much boring as it used to be in the early days. I assure you that you will not get a single moment to even think of getting bored.'

'Ya, I know this thing.'

They moved down the path, on both sides of which there was a never-ending farm, and in front of the path, there it was the double-storey house in the farmhouse.

'Why don't you also stay with us for two or three days? It will be great to have you here,' Uncle Borish asked Williams, opening the door for Williams and Jonathan.

'I have a flight to catch tomorrow, and it will be a long series of trips for me, approximately for two months. I will move to the city tomorrow with the sunrise.'

'As you wish,' Uncle Borish said and asked Williams and Jonathan to sit on the couch.

'You have maintained this farmhouse very well, Borish,' Williams appraised, looking around the room.

'Thank you, Mr. Bradman. It's been an honor serving your family and maintaining this farmhouse.'

'Come here, Jonathan. Let me show you your new room.'

Jonathan moved towards Uncle Borish who was holding the gate of a room, which he was about to open. As Jonathan got closer to the room, Borish opened it for him. It was small room with a single window that opened into the stable. Instead of the table and the bed, the whole room was empty.

'This room is the first to get the sunrays in the morning,' Uncle Borish said, opening the window.

'Don't you have any other room?' Jonathan asked.

'This is the best room for you, and don't forget, my son, at farmhouse, we have resources up to necessity,' Williams said.

'Why, God, why?' Jonathan murmured.

It was the first morning for Jonathan in the farmhouse, and as said by Uncle Borish, the first sunrays were directly falling upon his head. A knock on door wiped out Jonathan's remaining dream.

'Good morning, my son. The cattle are hungry,' Uncle Borish said, removing the holed curtains from the window.

'Why can't someone sleep late in a farmhouse?' Jonathan said with laziness and frustration, yawning into the bed.

'I think that's why it is called a farmhouse.'

The day for Jonathan started with feeding the cattle, taking them on a ride, checking the windmill. Binding the bundles of wheat and grains, and at last, checking the warehouse for space.

Jonathan went into the warehouse that was lighted only by the sunrays coming from the stepper gaps at the ceiling made of wooden planks and it was quite big. It was like a hall with a long path alongside of which huge bundles of tied hay were kept. Uncle Borish said Jonathan to check in the warehouse whether there is enough space for a new lot or not.

Moving deeper into the warehouse, Jonathan found an empty place at the right-hand side corner of the warehouse where old used parts of farmhouse machineries like tractor, cultivator, sprayer, and mower were kept. Jonathan moved on to check those rusted things and started throwing them in the corner after checking it for use, and suddenly Jonathan's eyes stuck at a thing, the presence of which in the warehouse of Uncle Borish's farmhouse was very much unexpected.

It was a plectrum with a caption 'Blood & Night' and a sign of half blade form that blood was trickling down. It was a cult pick that Jonathan had never seen in the market or anywhere else. It was a pick with self-explanatory story of legacy and death. The plectrum was wrapped in a transparent plastic. Jonathan took the pick into his pocket and started working in the warehouse.

The day was very much exhausting and frustrating for Jonathan. One after another, the tasks at the farmhouse were being served by Uncle Borish to Jonathan. Jonathan didn't hate visiting the farmhouse, but without his gear and a total mess with his whole two months' plan at music, it was creating the hatred. With the dawn when Jonathan was totally exhausted, the work ended. Finally he was with Uncle Borish on the dining table.

'So how was your first day at farmhouse?' Uncle Borish asked, taking the first sip of soup.

'Well, it was exhausting, frustrating, irritating, and—'

'Okay, okay, I understood. You will start loving this place, these cattle, this windmill, this house, and specially me,' Uncle Borish said and laughed.

'It's not like that, Uncle Borish. I don't hate you, I just hate this place because it keeps me away from my guitar, from my friends, and—'

'Hey, talking about friends. One of your friends from the city called and said to inform you that he will be arriving here tomorrow.'

'Friend of mine, here, when?' Jonathan exclaimed.

'I think he said tomorrow and his name was Mendis.'

'This is seriously awesome, Mendis coming to farmhouse. Now not even a single moment of mine will be bored to death.'

Mendis was Jonathan's school friend with whom he got to know about music. The whole family of Mendis was related to music. His mother was a piano player at a five-star restaurant and his father used to play in the navy band as a synth player. As a child, Jonathan always used to visit Mendis's house where there were a number of music instruments. Whenever Jonathan visited, Mendis always used to put an album of famous bands. Mendis was a very good bagpiper player, which he learned from his grandmother. Mendis was a skinny, tall guy with blond hair and was having spots of pimple all over his cheek for which he was always concerned about but was not able to get rid of. Families of both Jonathan and Mendis were known to each other, and Mendis's father was a good friend of Williams.

'Ya, but don't think that I will let you miss your daily work routine.'

'Don't worry, Uncle Borish, we will share the work. By the way, I found something very odd in the warehouse. Do you know whom does it belongs to?' Jonathan said and took out the pick from his pocket.

'Where did you find this? And did you remove the plastic cover?' Uncle Borish asked rudely.

'I found it in the warehouse, and I didn't remove the cover. But what's the matter?'

Uncle Borish took the pick into his hand and stared at it for a second.

'It is a pick, Uncle Borish. It is used to play guitar. And as per I know, no one in the farmhouse is related to music or guitar.'

Uncle Borish was still looking at the pick and acting like a deaf to whatever Jonathan was saying.

'Uncle Borish, Uncle Borish, are you listening?'

'Ya, ya. No, I don't know to whom does this pick belongs to,' Uncle Borish said and got up from the table.

'You haven't finished yet.'

'You carry on. I am feeling a bit tired. I am going to sleep. Good night.'

Uncle Borish left the pick on the table and stepped towards his room on the upper floor. Jonathan took the pick and looked at it with curiosity.

'Don't forget to close the door before going to bed,' Uncle Borish shouted from the first floor.

'Yes, Uncle.'

Someone early in the morning poured a bucket of water on Jonathan, and Jonathan jumped off from bed. He saw Mendis standing in the corner and laughing.

'Ha ha. I don't think you will need to take a bath today,' Mendis said, laughing.

'What the hell,' Jonathan said in frustration, looking at the wet bed and his wet clothes, and suddenly he ran towards Mendis who tackled him.

'Mendis, I will not leave you for this,' Jonathan shouted and ran towards Mendis who opened the main gate and ran towards the farm. Jonathan in his night dress started chasing Mendis into the farm.

After a long run, they both got exhausted and stopped at hay bundles.

'How the hell are you going to spend two months in this boring place?' Mendis panted, sitting on the hay bundle.

'I don't know. This farmhouse used to be a little interesting place at childhood, but now it looks like a dull, boring place,' Jonathan puffed.

'But I don't think Uncle Borish will give you a second to think of anything other than the work at farmhouse.'

'It's not his fault. He is very much connected to this farmhouse and he wants me to be fit. And the only way of being fit in farmhouse is to keep on working.'

'Then why don't we run away from here?'

'What? Run away from here? Are you mad?' Jonathan gasped, jumping off from the bundles.

'No. Who is asking to run? I am asking for a trip.'

'And you think my father would allow that.'

'Who needs the allowance? Uncle Borish is a good man,' Mendis said and they both smiled, looking at each other.

'You have been my savior from my childhood,' Jonathan said.

They both knew that if Jonathan's father would come to know that they have gone on a trip by escaping his well-planned farmhouse vacation, then Jonathan will be in some serious trouble.

'He is Mendis, Uncle Borish,' Jonathan said to Uncle Borish who was repairing his mower.

'I know. I was the one who sent him into your room,' Uncle Borish said, fitting the last nut into the bolt.

'Uncle Borish, I was thinking . . .'

'Think after we come from the village market,' Uncle Borish cut off Jonathan.

'So we all are going?'

'Yes. Get ready in ten minutes. I am taking the van out.'

'We will tell him on the way,' Mendis said, moving towards the farmhouse for changing dress.

'Don't you think we should wait a little, because you have just arrived and now we are leaving. It would leave a bad impression of yours on Uncle Borish.'

'You care about my impression or your farmhouse imprisonment? Because the more I will stay here, the more Uncle Borish will get used to us and will try to make us stay,' Mendis said, taking a shirt out of his luggage for Jonathan who was finding the right hole of his belt.

'At some point you are also right.'

'Hurry up, boys. The fresh vegetables would be sold in the market if we will get late,' Uncle Borish shouted from the main door.

'Coming, Uncle Borish.'

Uncle Borish was sitting at the front seat with Jonathan and Mendis on his left side. It was a good carrying van and the sound of empty tins kept at the back of the van was getting louder with every bump on the road.

'So you were saying something,' Uncle Borish asked from Jonathan, controlling the staring with one hand and keeping the other on the window for comfort.

'Yes, Uncle Borish, No, no, nothing important,' Jonathan mumbled and Mendis pinched him from the back.

They were into the vegetable market, which was very much crowded, and the noise of bargaining was tearing the place apart. Uncle Borish was checking out a big pumpkin for its freshness and Jonathan and Mendis were behind him, holding the already-filled bags of vegetables in both of their hands. Mendis whispered to Jonathan, 'Why the hell are you so much scared? He is not a giant monster who will eat you.'

'Every time I look into his eyes, all my courage wipes out.'

'It means I will have to say.'

'No, you will not, and I can't do this.'

'What, what you can't do?' Uncle Borish asked Jonathan as the whispering got louder.

'Nothing, nothing, Uncle Borish,' Jonathan said and kicked Mendis on his leg.

They were now loading the bags of vegetables and suddenly Mendis pushed Jonathan towards Borish.

'Yes, Jonathan,' Uncle Borish asked, seeing Jonathan stepping towards him.

'Aaah, the vegetables were very fresh,' Jonathan said with a smile and ran back.

They were on their way back to the farmhouse and Mendis was continuously pinching Jonathan to say and suddenly Jonathan shouted, 'Uncle Borish, we are going on a trip and then we will stay at one of our friends' house for two months.'

Uncle Borish stopped the car with a jerk.

'What? A trip?'

'Yes, we both are going on a trip for more than a month,' Jonathan said like a rapid fire.

'And it must be Mendis's plan,' Uncle Borish said, glaring at Mendis.

'No, it's a unite plan.'

'How can you even think of a trip, and how can you think that I will give an allowance to it? Your father will kill me for this.'

'Only if he gets to know this,' Jonathan said with a smile.

'Have you gone mad? You will go on a trip for more than a month and I will pretend to your dad that you are still here in the farmhouse?'

'Please, Uncle Borish, please. I don't want to spoil my maturity here.' Jonathan and Mendis both started begging with joined hands.

'Sit quietly and let's go back to farmhouse. You are getting out of control.'

'But, Uncle Borish—'

'Not a single word now,' Uncle Borish thundered and started the van.

All three were sitting on the dining table. Jonathan and Mnedis were eating with a paralyzed face and were acting like in a way that their homes had collapsed in flood, their mothers were hanging at a dam, their fathers were still missing, and they are diseased with an HIV-positive.

'Soup?' Uncle Borish asked Jonathan, passing the bowl of soup, and Jonathan looked at Borish with the most emotionally blackmailing face and nodded his head. Mendis tapped Jonathan's back as he nodded his head for soup.

Finally Uncle Borish took a deep breath and asked, 'So where are you planning for the trip?'

'Brasilia,' Mendis snapped.

'And for how long?'

'Two months.'

'Only you two?'

'Other friends will meet us at the spot.'

'Okay, so it was well planned. But I will not assure you that your dad will not come to know about this, but I will try my best.'

'We love you, Uncle Borish,' Jonathan said, jumping off from his chair, and they both hugged Uncle Borish tightly.

CHAPTER FIVE

THE JUNGLES OF AMAZON

Both of them were waiting at the main gate for the bus with their backpacks, and Uncle Borish was looking out for the bus by leaning out from the gate.

'I don't know why I am doing this, but please return home safely,' Uncle Borish said.

'Don't worry, Uncle. We will take care of each other and we will always be thankful for your kindnesses.'

'It's nothing like that. I can't see pale faces, and oh, here comes the bus.'

The bus stopped at the main gate because of Uncle Borish's waving hand. It was an old rusted bus filled with farmers, kittens, hens, and goats.

'Have a safe and nice journey,' Uncle Broish said, waving goodbye as the bus left the place.

'So we are going to Brasilia?' Jonathan asked Mendis, making himself fit in the small seat with hens at the left.

'No, my dear friend, we are going to Manaus, Brazil.'

'What, are you crazy? But we said that we were going to Brasilia.'

'Lies, lies, and lies, and if it makes your trip awesome, it will be forgiven by Jesus, my child. I knew that your uncle will never let us go to Manaus, so I had to.'

'And all our friends are dummy members?'

'Now you have started understating me,' Mendis said and smiled, looking at the window.

All the things were pre-planned by Mendis. He had already booked the tickets, hotels, tourist guide for the trip. Mendis was a savior for Jonathan from his childhood. Whenever Jonathan was in problem, Mendis was standing with him. Jonathan always felt lucky to have a friend like Mendis.

They got off the bus, took the flight, and flew away for the jungles of Amazon. The glee on their faces was unmatchable.

They were now into the city Manaus. It was a crowded place with modern concrete buildings and the place was full of tourists. People were packing backpacks for going into the jungle, preparing themselves for beaches. The place was full of greenery and spectacular views.

'Do you know that this city is known as the heart of Amazon?' Mendis asked Jonathan, crossing the busy street with a map in hand.

'No, I didn't know that, but one thing I know that you don't know where the hotel is.'

'Ah! Here it is.'

The hotel was just in front of them. It was already booked by Mendis through his debit card, which used to be always filled with money and the transaction of which was never questioned by his parents.

It was an average-looking hotel with a well-furnished reception, and a man in loose trousers, smoking cigarette, was standing behind it.

'Let me check,' the receptionist said, staring suspiciously at both of them.

'Here, the keys, room number 345,' the old receptionist said, handing over a rusted twin keys.

'Thank you,' Jonathan said, taking the key and smiling back.

'No drinking, no girls, no fighting,' the old man said, holding Jonathan's hand.

'Okay,' Jonathan said and wriggled away his hands from the old man's grab.

They were in front of the room 345. Jonathan took the key and opened it. The room was much more than what Mendis paid for, and it was just because of the spectacular view from the balcony, otherwise the room was very simple with a small television in a corner, double bed with cream-colored quilt, which looked like it used to be white at the start, a small table near the bed with a landline phone, a pot on it with dead flowers, and just in front of the bed there was a big framed poster of a village at dawn with mountains and rainfall.

'This is seriously awesome. We have a balcony. Jonathan, come and see the view,' Mendis said, running towards the balcony.

'Oh my god,' Jonathan said with excitement, seeing the spectacular view.

From the balcony, the whole city was visible. With modern concrete building to the long trees and the beach that was very far from the hotel.

'Brazil!' Mendis shouted, leaning out of the railing.

'So what are our plans for tomorrow?' Jonathan asked, jumping on to the bed.

'At first we will go to Paraque do Mindu, the Amazon opera house, then Encontro das Aguas where the black water meets the white water, and at last we will go to the marketplace for some shopping.'

'How can you remember these names?' Jonathan said, looking surprisingly at Mendis.

'As I said, planning is not a one-night work.'

'I thought that your father loved a Brazilian lady,' Jonathan said, moving slowly from the bed, and Mendis ran behind him.

The next day went in the same way as it was planned. They toured to most of the famous places of Manaus, and till dawn, they were at the main market. Although most of the buildings of Manaus were modern and were of concrete, the places outside the city still stored the culture of wood-framed buildings and shanty towns. Even the main market was a gothic-style place with high-reaching stained glass window. The economical condition of Brazil could be seen on a rise caused by the coffee boom.

On the next day, they were having a plan to spend five days into the jungles of Amazon by contacting an Amazon tour guide. It was the basic reason why Mendis chose to tour Manaus. He was very much fascinated by the jungles of Amazon and its stories about people getting lost in the jungles or no one ever has been able to cross the jungles of Amazon. It was away from the fact that now the tour of Amazon by most of the guides or tour companies are taken up to a limit and with all safety measures. But Mendis booked a guy for the other way around. The guy took Mendis and Jonathan deeper into the jungle, away from the regular path of tourists. The jungle of Amazon was looking like a live picture, which Jonathan and Mendis had seen only in documentaries. They could hear animal life all over the place. The dense forest of Amazon was making the trip adventurous as well as swelling an essence of fear in both of them. Animals were howling and screaming, path was becoming more unpredictable, every step, every touch on wood for support was being firstly assured for no any presence of life-threatening animals like snake, scorpion, spider, and many more. The sound of river flow was continuing throughout the path because they were going nearby it. The river used to become a giant whenever it rained, and people of Amazon used to say that rain has true love for Amazon, and since both are immortal, they will never leave each other.

It was their third day in the jungles. The sun was just on the way to hide and rest. They were searching for three pairs of trees that were close to each other so that they could tie their temporary hanging sleeping arrangement with it. It also served as a protection from animals and insects as it was at some distance from the ground. Jonathan and the guide were just on the verge of finishing the set-up while Mendis was sitting on the ground and looking at the small portion of sky visible in between the trees.

'Go and search for some dry wood, we need fire at night,' the guide said, making the knot.

'Jonathan, would you like to come?' Mendis asked Jonathan.

'I am not yet finished.'

'The woods must be good. Search for some dry ones,' the guide said, giving a sudden pull at his last knot.

CHAPTER SIX

PINCH POINT

The night was even more haunting in the Amazon. At daytime, one could at least get assured about the animals, but at night, it was all like a surprise, a bad surprise. It looked like the animals loved threatening the visitors at night as much as the guide loved Mendis's cross bracelet. Looking into the darkness, one could only wish to get attacked by a small animal. Jonathan was still trying to close his eyes and was avoiding looking in the dark for a giant. But Mendis and the guide were sleeping in the way that they were at some five-star hotel on a comfortable bed and pillow, and an air conditioner just at the right temperature.

Jonathan always used to have this problem of sleeping. The only safe place for Jonathan to sleep was with his mom or Sivur around. Other than that, every place in the world used to be a challenge for Jonathan to sleep. After trying for an hour, when Jonathan's eyes started to blur, suddenly he heard some whispering. He woke up and looked towards Mendis and the guide. They were still sleeping with irritating snorting. Jonathan looked here and there but found no one around. He slowly lay back on the hanging bed and again the whispering came from the right-hand side. It looked like two men were gossiping very slowly. Jonathan got up from his bed and took a wood from the fire in his hand, the tip of which was still burning and was enough to look through the darkness. He didn't find it important to wake up any of them and stepped into his shoes. The night was blood-curdling, and with very limited visibility, animals howling, the place was looking more treacherous. He slowly and steadily started stepping towards the whispering that was getting louder and louder. Shortening his cornea, Jonathan tried to look into the darkness. His heartbeat was increasing and the whispering was getting louder when suddenly someone tapped Jonathan from the back and he screamed.

'Goddamn, Mendis, you scared me,' Jonathan said in alarm, looking at Mendis and pushing him behind.

'I scared you? Where the hell are you going with this flambeau?'

'Hsssh, listen and hold it,' Jonathan whispered.

As they stepped forward, a purple light started coming from the front. A source of such a bright light at that time of night in the jungles of Amazon was, no doubt, mysterious and furious.

'We should call the guide,' Mendis whispered.

'Just shut up and move,' Jonathan snapped.

Following the light and sound that were getting shiner and louder, they reached at a point from where it looked like all the things were behind a giant tree.

'I think there is an alien,' Mendis said, hiding behind the tree.

'Some new animal,' Jonathan whispered.

'Who shines purple and whispers like men.'

'There is only one way to find out.'

'We will do it on a count.'

'Wait, there is something on the tree,' Mendis said, holding Jonathan's hand who was just about to move.

'Bring the fire here,' Jonathan asked Mendis.

Mendis brought the fire near the tree and Jonathan shortened his cornea to read it.

'PINCH POINT.'

Mendis read it out for Jonathan, and as Jonathan heard it, he stepped backward with surprise and gaped.

'This can't be real. It's a dream,' Jonathan mumbled and touched the written letters.

'What are you doing? Someone would have written it. What's so surprising in this?'

'No, no. You are not getting it. It is the same thing what Sivur told me in his stories of Riffsland.'

'Sivur? How does Sivur come in the picture?' Mendis questioned, and suddenly there came a sound of a group of horses riding towards them.

'Someone is coming,' Jonathan said and pushed Mendis down to hide.

They saw seven to eight men on horses that went behind the tree. Due to the darkness, neither their face nor their clothes was visible. Jonathan leaned from the tree to look what was there and he was stunned. Mendis shook him, asking, 'What is there?' but Jonathan was acting like a statue and suddenly Mendis also got up and leaned from the tree. Then he found out why Jonathan went numb.

It was a huge gate, twenty to thirty feet high, in the middle of the jungle, which was shining bright purple. It was looking like the gate was made of glass and thousands of long lighting purple threads were fit into the gate. The men on horse were standing near the door and were just looking at it.

'What the hell is this?' Jonathan murmured.

'It is here,' one of the men on the horse said.

Due to the bright light, those men's faces and clothes were still not visible.

'We need to get in before he gets away,' another man on the horse said.

Suddenly, one of the men tapped his horse to move near the gate and he banged the gate with something in his hand, which enlightened a bolt in the gate, and all of a sudden everyone in front of the door started getting pushed towards it due to a very powerful force coming out of the gate. The force was so strong that even the small trees started losing their grip on the ground. A strong wind from the door started engulfing everything in front of it. All the horsemen got sucked by the gate while Jonathan and Mendis were still holding the giant tree and were waving in the air like a leaf in a tornado.

'What the hell is this?' Jonathan shouted as he started losing grip on the trunk of the tree.

'Keep holding, don't lose the grip,' Mendis squealed and suddenly he lost the hold on the trunk and got engulfed by the gate.

Jonathan shouted, 'Mendis!' and he too got into the gate.

Both Jonathan and Mendis fell on a rocky base.

'Where the hell are we?' Mendis said, holding his head that banged due to the fall.

He helped Jonathan to get up and stepped a little forward to see where they were and suddenly Jonathan stopped Mendis from stepping forward as he saw a dead end. They were on a cliff of a rocky mountain, and the depth from the edge where they were standing was nearly more than a thousand foot and covered with fog.

'How the hell we got here? Is this some kind of magic trick?' Mendis said, looking at the sky.

They were not able to believe what had just happened to them when suddenly the horsemen, who were in the jungle and standing near the gate, came from the other side of the mountain.

'They are the one,' Jonathan murmured, looking at the horsemen.

Now in the daylight they were able to see the horsemen. They were looking scary with long beard and hairs. They were wearing baggy dresses made from animal skin and their horses were painted with different colors and very mesmerizing art was drawn on their skin. They were big, at least for Jonathan and Mendis.

'Who the hell are you?' one of the horsemen asked Jonathan.

'I don't know how we got here, please let us go in our city, we will not harm anyone,' Mendis begged.

'We are the Gorams, kill them both,' the horseman said, and suddenly another horseman took a guitar hanging on his back.

Jonathan had never seen such a tremendous guitar in his life. It was a little rusted, but the artwork and the wings at its neck left Jonathan and Mendis both speechless. As he took it in his hand, it turned into a long sharp sword, which was looking half as guitar. He tapped his horse and started coming closer towards both of them. Jonathan and Mendis stepped backwards and stopped at the edge with never-ending depth behind them.

Out of the blue, the man on the horse with sword in hand fell from his horse. An arrow hit his back and suddenly more horsemen came from the back side of these horsemen. They were shouting, well dressed, and looking more sophisticated.

All the Gorams turned backwards towards those shouting horsemen and started moving violently towards them. They both clashed like two gigantic waves in an ocean, but those well-dressed horsemen were looking more powerful and were making the battle one-sided. The clashing of the weapons was producing sparks. They started chopping those Gorams one by one. Some of the Gorams threw plectrums towards them, which when reached near to the others, swelled black smoke, but as it reached near to them, they sliced the plectrums down with their weapons. Seeing this, some of the Gorams started running to save their life, but at the top of the mountain, there was only one way out, from where these horsemen came. Two of the Gorams jumped off from the cliff into the never-ending depth while most of them got killed in the battle. They captured two of them who were lying on the ground under their feet. As the war ended, their weapon started turning into heavy guitars, drumsticks, violins, and flutes.

'Tell me how the hell you opened the gate?' one of those from the winning side asked the two defeated ones, but they didn't open their mouth.

'This is not a good sign, they have opened the gate. We will carry them to the kingdom,' one of the well-dressed horsemen said.

'But how could this be possible?' another one said.

'Our world is not safe now. The Guttadevers will rise soon. We should inform The Three as soon as possible.'

'Who the hell are you?' one of them asked, when Jonathan and Mendis came into their notice, who were standing near the cliff and shivering.

'We don't belong to this place. Let us go,' Mendis begged.

One of the men came closer to Mendis and turned his head by holding his hair to look at his neck while both of them shivered with fear.

'No, he is not one of them,' the man said, looking at Mendis's and Jonathan's necks.

'Take them to the kingdom,' another one said, and one of them held Jonathan and Mendis from the back and ordered them to move forward on different horses.

They all were having long hairs, some of them were tied, some unmanaged, and some of them were curly. Two of the horsemen were wearing a long cream-colored cloak, which was looking tremendous, and they both were identical with brown long hairs, which was well combed and tied with a ponytail at the back. The only difference between the two was the piercing in the ears of one of them. One of them little fat, bald, and was having beard, starting right from his ears, and was tied with curved pairs of steel. A rope tied at his tummy, which was holding his baggy dress. The variety of weapons that they were carrying was wide among them. Others were also wearing different-colored cloaks over the golden armory with tight pants and a hood at the back. The only odd one among them was the bald and fat one.

CHAPTER SEVEN

RIFFSLAND

They carried both of them all the way down to the mountain. From the top of the mountain, the ground was not visible due to fog, but as they started going down, they realized that the depth was much more than what they imagined. All the way down to the mountain was a steeper one-way path or halfway path because even the horses were not able to adjust themselves on the steeper roads and were moving slowly. Sometime the horses used to slip a little at the edge, but nothing could be seen from the reaction of those horsemen. Even a brick would have better expression than their faces.

Down the valley, it was all rocky base, most of the part of which was still covered with fog. Visibility was only up to four to five feet, but still they were moving very fast and looked like they knew each small piece of the way to their destiny or what they called as kingdom. The fog was so dense that other than their horse, nothing was visible. Only their tapping could be heard, which looked like they were seven to eight in numbers. Moving on the way, sitting at the back of one of the horsemen, Jonathan's eyes stuck at the drumsticks hanging at the horseman who was carrying him. It was the same drumstick that got converted into that bow and arrow from which he saved Jonathan's life. It was like a dream for Jonathan, and suddenly Jonathan murmured, 'Riffsland.'

No, no, this is not possible. How could a story come true? The Pinch Point, these instruments converting into weapon, this can't be true, Jonathan thought.

'You all are shredder and legends from the city Riffsland?' Jonathan said to the horseman riding him, but the sound was loud enough to be heard by all the horsemen, and as they heard Jonathan, all of them stopped. The horsemen threw a sharp glare at Jonathan. He jumped off from his horse and pulled Jonathan down harshly on the ground.

'Who told you about Riffsland?' he thundered, putting a knife onto his neck, which he took out from his pocket.

'It's a story told by my servant,' Jonathan said, crawling back.

'Don't lie to me, tell me who told you. These Gorams?' he asked again and pushed Jonathan's leg towards him.

'I don't know any Gorams. We got engulfed by the gate. But I have heard this story about your city.'

'Move aside, he is scared,' another horseman came from the fog and the one holding Jonathan moved aside. His dress was different from the others. It was a red Jerkin and with no artwork on it, but only with a symbol on both sides. The symbol was of a guitar at center and two snakes on both of its side. He was in tight pants and long leather boots. Both of his hands were filled with golden bracelet. His face was thin and pointed at the chin. He had dark black curly hairs. A pigeon's feather was hanging from his left ear through a golden thread.

'My name is George Flippin. If you will tell the truth, no one will hurt you, but if you will lie in front of The Three, I will shove this knife in your neck.'

'But—' Jonathan tried to say something, but George cut him off.

'We will talk in the kingdom. Take him back on the horse.'

Jonathan was not able to see on which horse Mendis was or he was there or not.

After a long ride when the fog got cleared, Jonathan saw the most mesmerizing view of his life. It was a huge castle, which was still very far from where they were standing. Far in the fog, there was a palace in the castle that looked like hanging in clouds. The castle was separated by a long and wide river in front of them over which a long bridge was there. Jonathan knew that this is the city Riffsland that Sivur used to tell him in his stories.

Jonathan was now able to see the other horsemen riding with him and he also saw Mendis on one of the horses with another horseman. He knew that talking or signaling anything to Mendis would not be a good step. So he just looked at him and nodded his head.

They were now near the bridge, which was much longer than it looked. The bridge was upon the river, which was parting the castle from the rocky mountain and land from where they came.

When Jonathan looked down at the bridge, he realized that it was a fret of a guitar. Jonathan thought, 'Why did Sivur never tell me anything about this?' The bridge was very long and it took nearly half an hour to cross that bridge because they were moving very slowly on it.

They were finally at the main gate, which was already opened for them. The doors of the gate, which were made of wood, were carved with awe-inspiring art. Two men in armory were holding the long wooden plank that was holding the gate. They looked quite surprised to see Jonathan and Mendis coming along with the horsemen. They entered into the castle through the main gate and now they were inside it. The castle started with the marketplace, which was very much crowded, but the passage for passing horses was being given by them without any difficulty. It was looking like a common market, with most of the ladies in prairie dress while dresses of men varied from leather jackets, cloak, to sleeveless baggy outfits and full-sleeved white shirts. In the market, fruit, vegetables, crockery, dresses, and many other things were being sold. The buildings were made of limestone and were looking very close to old architecture with windows of stained glasses and every house was having a chimney at its terrace. As Jonathan, Mendis, and the two other captured horsemen came into their notice, they started whispering among themselves and everyone was glaring at them. It looked like unexpected visitors were not welcomed in the castle. The marketplace was about to end, and in front of the end of the marketplace, there it was, the palace hanging in clouds.

The palace was hanging in the sky on the white cloud, which was acting as a base for it. The only thing connecting the palace with the ground was a long flight of stairs that was starting from the ground and ending into the clouds. On each stair, there were different staff notes carved very beautifully. The pillars of the palace were wrapped in climber plants, and in the middle of the pillars, there was a long wooden gate. The horsemen got off from their horses and tied them with a wooden plank, which were many in numbers. In those series of wooden planks, there were a number of tied horses. The one in the red cloak ordered the others to tie their hands with the rope given by the fat man. Jonathan, Mendis, and the two Gorams were now tied and were following those cloaked ones to the stairs. With every step, the height of stairs from the ground was increasing and was making the way to the palace frightening. Jonathan somehow dared to move a little towards the edge and looked what's below the stairs. Expecting ground or something related, what Jonathan saw made him speechless. It was a gigantic waterfall, falling from a mountain filled with greenery. Even from such a height, the sound of water falling from the mountain and clashing with the ground could be heard. The whole place was filled with greenery with some very colorful flowers, trees, and animals also. The view was tremendous. The river, which was starting from the waterfall, was leading under the ground from where it seemed to get lost.

Jonathan stepped backwards, looked at Mendis, swallowed, and nodded his head. Crossing the long stairs now, they were in front of the wooden gate. George stepped towards the gate and touched it. He whispered some words by getting closer to the gate and suddenly he got vanished.

'What was that?' Mendis gasped.

'Blink your eyes and you will be there,' the fat one said.

And suddenly Jonathan also vanished from there, and when Mendis turned backwards, he also got vanished.

They were now into a dark jungle, and in front of them, there was a big, really big tree with wide trunk. George was kneeling in front of the big tree when suddenly the big tree spoke.

'So they are the one.'

He was speaking with the big mouth at the middle of the trunk. He was having two eyes and a nose at the middle. It was looking like a human tree.

'Father, they have broken the gate and no one knows how. We captured two Gorams and we don't have any idea about these two kids,' George said to the tree.

'Oh, it's a bad news. You can take them to the kingdom,' the tree said and stared at Jonathan.

'You will have to spend a long time here,' the tree said to Jonathan and disappeared. Again it became a common giant tree with no any face.

'Thank you, Father,' George said and again they were at the gate that started opening slowly.

'Who was he?' Mendis murmured.

'He is the father. He is the one. We always take suggestion from him and everybody says that he knows all the things. After so many years, the gate which was controlled by The Three has been broken by the Gorams with you. From his woods, all the instruments in Riffsland have been made. But only few can talk to him, like The Three, members of Wargskult, and George. By the way, my name is Zoran, Zoran Didli,' the fat one said to Mendis.

The gate opened and they entered into a big open area in which there were a number of men with a particular instrument hanging at their back in cloaks, red, blue, black armory, tight pants, pointed shoes, and long hairs, either sitting, standing, or roaming here and there. As George, Zoran, Jonathan, Mendis with two Gorams passed by those group of men, everyone passed a strange look at them. In front of the open area, two stairs, one from right and one from left, were leading to a single opened gate. At the left and right side of the open area, there were a number of stairs that were also leading to some opened gates, but the gate in front was looking of utter most importance due to its artwork, stained glasses, and marvelous gems carved into its walls. There was a symbol above the gate in the middle. It was a symbol of a tree with two beehives. There were three branches of the tree of white, black, and blue color that were holding the two beehives, which were black and white in color, respectively. There were five hexagons in both beehives, which were together making the beehives.

Zoran took the Gorams to the left-hand side stairs, which were leading to another gate, while George and another took Jonathan and Mendis to the stairs in front of them. They took the right-hand side stairs and entered into the main gate. The gate was leading to a long hallway, the roof of which was made of stained glasses from which sprinkled sunrays were passing by. The hallway ended into a corridor. There were a number of gates in the corridor, and one was just in front of them. They stepped towards that gate that led them to a big hall in which there was a very long dining table at the middle and an awe-inspiring chandelier just above it.

'Have you informed them?' George asked from one of his mates.

'Yes. They are on their way.'

Instead of George, all his mates with whom he went on to the rocky hills to kill Gorams left the room. Now in the big hall, only George, Jonathan, and Mendis were left. George moved to the extreme right corner of the table and stood behind the chair in front of him, while Jonathan and Mendis were just behind him. Number of footsteps started coming from the other side of the room. They were moving steadily and fast than usual speed.

Three old men entered into the hall. Two of them were in long embroidered doublet while the middle one was in embroidered tunic. One of them was longer than the other two and was in the middle. He was having white curly hairs that extended up to his waist at back. His beard was long and white and his full-sleeved embroidered tunic was black in color with golden embroidered collar. His face was bigger and was matching with his height. He was looking very curiously at Jonathan and Mendis. The one in the left was in dark blue embroidered doublet, extending up to his knees, with big black buttons and was without any collar. He was having straight but short golden brown hairs, extending only up to his neck. He was having many rings, bracelets in his fingers and hands, and was a little fat. The leather of his shoes was looking like the skin of a bat, and the last one who was in white long embroidered doublet was having beard only below his lips, which was long, straight, tied, and white in color. His hairs were curly too and were dark black. They were The Three. Valdus Lehmington in black, Zorich Plutos in blue, and Rother Fredman in white embroidered doublet dress.

'The Three,' Jonathan murmured.

As they entered into the hall, George bowed down in front of them and they took the three seats at the table.

'So they are the two,' Valdus asked, straightening his long beard.

'Yes, Sir Valdus,' George answered politely.

'And what about the Gorams?' Rother asked, getting up from his chair and coming closer to Jonathan and Mendis.

'Five of them were killed on the spot and two have been captured.'

'The gate was last opened in the battle by the Gorams, since then it has never been opened by them. The gate which was controlled by us mostly for the recruiters has been broken by these Gorams. It's not a good sign. Send our messenger to the four directions and inform the Prime Ones that the evil will rise again,' Rother said, putting his hand on his forehead.

'What about these kids, sir? One of them said that he knows about our kingdom and everything related to it.'

'Which one?' Valdus asked.

'Me, Sir Valdus. My servant always used to tell me this story of Riffsland, You three—the creator—Wargskult, Guttadavers, their members, the fest, and everything,' Jonathan mumbled.

'And how did you get here?' Valdus questioned him.

'We were on a trip in the jungles of Amazon and suddenly we saw a purple light coming from the jungle. Just in a second, these horsemen arrived and one of them hit the gate due to which everything near the gate got engulfed by it. We too,' Mendis mumbled.

Sir Zorich was continuously looking at Mendis and was not saying anything.

'So you mean to say that it was not intentional,' Rother said.

'Yes.'

'A common boy from other world having the knowledge of our kingdom is not a good sign,' Rother said to Valdus.

'It's not surprising. From so many years, these abandoned Gorams are outside our world. In order to destroy our kingdom, they must have been telling the secret of our world to common men. And from one to another, it has spread like a virus,' Valdus said.

'But what about the black strip of bond?' Rother questioned.

'It is lost. So we can't say anything about it. Lock these children in chamber 675. We will let them go into their world tomorrow. They have no any business here,' Valdus said, got up, and moved towards the gate, while Rother and Valdus were still there.

'But what about my servant and his stories? I have been hearing about all of you from my childhood. I want to know why," Jonathan begged as George held both of them from their collar.

'Are you mad? Is it not enough that they are letting us go from here?' Mendis whispered, coming closer to Jonathan.

But Rother and Valdus didn't speak a word and just kept looking at Jonathan who was being dragged by George.

'Don't create a problem for me or I will return it with interest,' George snapped, pushing Jonathan and Mendis into the chamber 675 and smashing the door.

CHAPTER EIGHT

BLOOD SHREDDER

The chamber was small with an old bench made of limestone at the left. The only source of light was the small window at the gate with rusted iron bars. The walls were very much rough and so was the floor. It was not a good place to pass even a single night.

'Thank God. Now tomorrow we will go from here.' Kneeling down, Mendis thanked God.

'This is not the right way, Mendis. I will break out tonight,' Jonathan said.

'No no. You will not do this. Everything is going fine. They will leave us tomorrow and now you want to spoil everything?' Mendis growled.

'We will go in our world and then what, our boring day-to-day life. I have been hearing this story from my childhood. I don't know whether some Gorams told them or what. But the thing about which I have been fantasizing from my childhood, I can't let it go like this.'

'So it means that believing on a story told by Sivur, we are going to risk our life here. I am not in the mood.'

'I am breaking out tonight. Are you coming or not?'

'You are a piece of rigid rock, Jonathan. But I assure you that you will regret your decision in the future.'

'You are my best friend, Mendis,' Jonathan said and hugged Mendis.

At night there were two guards at the gate. Jonathan and Mendis were acting to sleep. Looking at the guards through the gate, Jonathan signaled Mendis and he started howling by holding his stomach.

'Someone help. Please help!' Jonathan screamed.

A guard entered in a hurry by opening the door and took Mendis in his lap by kneeling down when suddenly Jonathan snatched the guitar hanging from the guard's back and all of a sudden it turned into a hammer. As it turned into a hammer, it fell due to its weight on the guard and he fainted. And from the back, a guard grabbed Jonathan and rammed him on the floor. Mendis pushed the guitar of the fainted guard, which was no more a hammer. The guitar slid towards Jonathan, and as he again held it in his hands, it turned into a hammer, and by completing a 180-degree rotation, it banged the guard grabbing Jonathan.

'How do you do this?' Mendis screamed as the hammer again turned into a guitar.

'This is freaking awesome. Let me try once more,' Jonathan said and moved towards the guitar.

But Mendis pushed him back, saying, 'We don't have time, let's move on.'

They stepped out of the door and it was a hallway with prisons at both of its side. At the first turn, the hallway was leading to two turns, one at the left and the other at the right. They took the right one. Suddenly a guard arrived due to the sound of the hammer that fell on the other guard at the prison. He looked at the opened gate and then at Jonathan and Mendis. He took out two drumsticks from his back, which were kept crossed to each other, and the two drumsticks turned into two medium-sized swords. He started running towards Jonathan and Mendis. Aiming perfectly, he threw one of the sword towards Jonathan, but Mendis pushed Jonathan away and the sword passed by an inch difference from Jonathan. Running madly, Jonathan looked at Mendis and thought, 'How I will thank you for saving my life for I don't know how many times.'

They started running in the opposite direction and the guard was getting near to them. They took sharp turns in the hallway but the guard was familiar with every inch of that place and suddenly another guard joined the chase, which made Jonathan and Mendis stop at a place with no any way to go and guards at both end. Jonathan looked at an open door on the left on which chamber number 631 was written.

Jonathan pushed Mendis into that door. Mendis grabbed Jonathan's collar, which made both of them fall beside the door. The room was pitch-dark, but Jonathan got up and ran towards the door to close it so that the guards couldn't enter into it. But the door was already locked.

'Where the hell are we?' Mendis said and the echo of the sound made them realize that the room was much bigger than their expectation.

'How could I know?' Jonathan said.

Suddenly flambeau started burning at both side of the room. They were leading to a long stone passageway. Looking at the size of the other rooms, the size of this room was like magic.

'Do we need to go?' Mendis murmured.

'We don't have any other option.'

Jonathan started moving slowly towards the passageway. It was long and was looking never ending. At both side of the passageway, flambeaus were burning aggressively. But after a long walk, Jonathan saw that there was a dead end because there was no way that was leading from there.

'It looks like a dead end,' Mendis said.

They both moved on towards the dead end. It was looking like a black wall, which was very uneven. Jonathan stepped slowly towards the wall, and as he touched it, a huge swarm of bats flew away from that place, which made Jonathan and Mendis fall on the ground. They both lay on the ground and closed their eyes. The swarm of bats was huge and they were flying with full speed. Finally the wave ended and Jonathan tried to look through his closed eyes whether the bats had gone or not. He stood up and looked forward, while Mendis was still on the ground with closed eyes and face.

'I said you not to come here. This is a freaking place. How easy it was, we were on the way to home by just sitting in that prison and waiting for the sunshine. But you wanted it another way and, Jonathan. Jonathan! Are you listening or not?' Mendis mumbled and got up to look where Jonathan was.

The view behind the wall of bats that flew away was mesmerizing. It was like a pond, but the water was still at the path without any glass or support. Jonathan moved towards the still water and touched it. A small part of it flew away in the air and got stuck at the roof. It was looking like the place was gravitation-free only for the water.

'Now what the hell is this,' Mendis drawled and touched the water and the same thing happened with him.

All of a sudden, Jonathan jumped into the water.

'Jonathan!' Mendis screamed and looked at the crystal-clear water, but Jonathan was not there. It made one thing sure that the place at which this water was much bigger.

'Why did I follow him?' Mendis said like he was going to cry and jumped into the water.

The water was crystal-clear, and he started going up from where a source of light was coming. Mendis tried to hold himself on the ground by swimming deep into the bottom but didn't find Jonathan anywhere. When he started losing his breath, he swum all the way up and found that the light was coming from a hole just above him. He held the side of the hole and tried to push himself up. A hand from above the hole came and pushed Mendis above the water. It was Jonathan.

'Don't ever try to leave me like this again.' Mendis panted.

'Look at this,' Jonathan drawled, pointing towards his back.

'Now what?' Mendis dinned.

There was a guitar at the center of lava on a piece of rock. The guitar was red covered in dust and more than half of its part was buried under the rock. The red color on the guitar was not looking like a painting. It was looking like someone's blood had sprout on it. It was without any string and was looking very heavy. The horns at the top of its neck and the sign of an angel's white feather at it was looking marvelous. But there was no way to get that guitar because of the burning lava around it.

'The Blood Shredder,' Jonathan murmured.

'The Blood Shredder?' Mendis questioned.

'Yes, it is,' Jonathan said and started stepping slowly towards the guitar.

He was not able to even move his eyes or let it blink from the guitar. The view of the Blood Shredder at the middle of burning lava buried in rock was mesmerizing.

'There is no way to the guitar,' Mendis shouted from where he was because he didn't want to get buried in that lava.

But Jonathan was moving towards the guitar like someone had hypnotized him. When Mendis found that Jonathan was very much close to the lava and was going to fall in it, he ran towards him, but from the sky, a witch in brown cloak with lower body part made of black smoke, head of a skull, and a crown at its head banged Mendis into the walls. Mendis tried to get up, but his vision got blurred and was not able to stand properly. The witch was just in front of him and was screaming loudly by looking at Mendis. On the other hand, as Jonathan put his step into the lava, little pieces from the rock at the center started making a path on the lava for Jonathan. Jonathan stepped on to that path and the rock after his each step were making the way clear for him. He got near the guitar and bent a little. As he touched the guitar, a crack appeared in the rock and a strong force of white light came from it which made Jonathan and Mendis almost blind. From the hole of water, Vladus, Rother, Zorich, and George came. They were also looking very much surprised at what was happening there. Due to the light, Jonathan fell on to the ground and the last thing that he saw was The Three and George running towards him.

CHAPTER NINE

THE UNTOLD STORY

With closed eyes, Jonathan found that he was lying on something, but he was not able to open his eyes. He heard someone saying, 'No, there is no way he could cross the Wall of Bat, Cursed Water, and the Crowned Witch.'

'But he was there at the Blood Shredder, and he was not only there, he broke the rock in which the guitar is buried,' another voice said.

'Who is this boy? From the past twenty years, no one has even found the chamber 631. It was hidden.'

'We need to bring the three powers and complete the Blood Shredder, because if we will not do so, Guttadevers will do it before us.'

'You are right. Zoran, call the Wargskult, send this message to all the four zones and we will bring back the Pick of Dragon, Buried Belt, and String of Snakes.'

Jonathan, after hearing this, lost his sense again, as he was already feeling very weak. After a while, when Jonathan found it okay to open his eyes, he looked up to see where he was. He was in a room, on the side of which a lamp was kept in which candles were burning. On the other side, in a plate, surgical items with a number of colorful small bottles were kept. It was for no doubt a first-aid room. Jonathan, thinking that he was alone in the room, got up and suddenly found that a big bald man, with only one eye, another one covered with leather strap, was sitting on a table near the door. He was having a big bass guitar on his back and was staring continuously at Jonathan.

Jonathan looked at the man, smiled but got no any reply from the other side, so he found it better to lie down on the bed again. He turned down towards Mendis and whispered, 'Mendis, Mendis.'

'No, I can't marry the witch, her mouth smells a lot,' Mendis mumbled in his sleep and suddenly someone rammed the door. It was George and Zoran.

'You saw the Blood Shredder and you also broke it. Tell me the truth, how did you pass the three most dangerous obstacles in Riffsland?' Zoran tried to ask rudely.

'I don't remember everything. It was having two horns and then the white light and I fainted,' Jonathan said, trying to get up from his bed.

'This is not a joke. You will have to answer The Wargskult and The Three about this. After Andrew Blake's death, no one has even got near to the Blood Shredder, but God knows how you got there and broke the rock,' George said furiously.

'Even I don't know how I got there. It was like some force calling me to get there,' Jonathan said.

'Everything will change. The news has spread like a virus in the city and this will not be hidden from Guttadevers also. You have changed everything and you will be answerable for it.'

As George finished his bunch of harsh words on Jonathan, who was still in shock, a very short-heighted man, little fat and bald with big nose and hairy hands, entered into the room in a hurry.

'Oh, I think I am late. The boy has woken up,' he said.

'No, Dimitri. You are not late. George was just showing the way he is,' a lady coming up from the walls said. And as she came out of the walls, her body started changing its color to normal, which was earlier just like the wall.

'That's why they call you the Lady of Camouflage, Miss Margret Blake,' George said.

'Blake, you are from the family of Andrew Blake and his wife, Isabel Blake,' Jonathan babbled.

'Looks like this boy has a lot of information about us. But this is not the way to talk to a small boy,' Margret said.

'I would like to spend some time with this boy. Alone,' George said, coming closer to Jonathan.

'I think we need to go, Jonathan. I have been ordered to take care of you until the members of Wargskult arrives,' Dimitri said, getting into the way of George.

'Don't stop me, Dimitri,' George said, pushing Dimitri away.

'Don't you think that overruling Valdus's order will be the biggest offense in Riffsland,' Margret said, holding George's hand.

'Come, Jonathan, come with me,' Dimitri said politely, helping Jonathan to get down from his bed.

'You will have to answer, Jonathan, each and everything,' George squealed as Dimitri took Jonathan out of the room by holding his hand.

'He is a good man, but what you did with the Blood Shredder has made him like this. The secret chamber number 631 is the thing of uttermost importance to him. And an unknown small kid from the other world broke it like a cakewalk. I was expecting this type of behavior from Gerorge,' Dimitri said, passing the hallway, holding Jonathan's hand.

'Can you please tell me everything about it? I think I know only a drop from the ocean,' Jonathan said.

'The things which you know are enough. A kid from the other world shouldn't know these things. You will have to answer about it tomorrow, when the members of Wargskult arrives.'

'But why they? Valdus is the rule maker. Everyone will accept what he will decide for me. And Rother and Zurich are also there. And please tell me, who is this lady Margret Blake?'

'But the matter of Blood Shredder has forced the members to come and see who is the one with so much courage and power? And Margret Blake is the sister of Isabel Blake who is still in her sleep.'

'Still in sleep?' Jonathan questioned.

'Looks like you don't know everything about Riffsland. These Gorams don't even know how to leak the secrets. They are so dumb. The Blood Shredder which you have already seen belonged to the lead guitarist of Wargskult, Andrew Blake. On the darkest night, his wife, Isabel Blake, gave all her powers into that guitar so that Andrew Blake can fight with full power. But as she transferred the power, she went weak. She told Andrew Blake that when he will return from the war, she will take the power back and will be all right again. But in the war, Andrew Blake was killed, and as Guttadevers reached to take the Blood Shredder, the guitar's power spread into three parts, the Pick of Dragon, Buried Belt, and the String of Snakes. It was done by Isabel Blake. She knew that if the Blood Shredder will be in the hand of Guttadevers, the whole Riffsland will be finished. But even after the death of Andrew Blake, Wargskult won the war. But when everyone returned from the war, Isabel Blake was in her longest sleep, which is still lasting. It is said that when Andrew Blake was killed, his guitar's power spread and as Isabel Blake said that she will be fine again only if the guitar will be returned to him. And when the Blood Shredder lost its power, she also lost her life and became a living dead body. Now when all the three powers will be brought back, she will wake up again from her twenty years of sleep. From the past twenty years, many troops, many masters have went on to the journey of finding these three powers, but only lucky ones have returned,' Dimitri said, passing a number of hallways, and finally entered into a balcony from which the whole city of Riffsland was visible. From even such a height, the city was still looking very big. Even in the late night, it was still bright out there with a lamp in every house. The view was marvelous and the cold breeze at the balcony was adding taste to the flavor.

'That's why the members of Wargskult have hid their instruments because it might happen that Guttadvers from so many years are on the search of these three powers, and if they will have all the three powers, the Blood Shredder will be theirs,' Jonathan guessed.

'Talking about the Guttadevers, there are many myths. Some say that they are still hiding because they lost their power in the battle, some say that they are on the search of the three powers, and some also say that they are transformed into soul and are being protected in grave and are waiting for the right time to come into their real body. But one thing is for sure, that they are still alive because they are immortal as the members of Wargskult also are. So this is your room,' Dimitri said, removing the blue curtains.

'If all of them are immortal, how did Andrew Blake die?'

'Because they became immortal after the power from Blood Shredder came out. It somehow made all the Prime Ones immortal.'

It was a very big room for a single person. A reading table with lamp, a double bed in the center, number of books kept in shelf at right, a dining table near the bed. Everything was there in the room. But instead of the room, Jonathan was still standing at the balcony and looking at the city.

'I have tried many a times to get a room near the balcony, but I am not that lucky,' Dimitri said, joining Jonathan at the balcony.

'I have been hearing the story of Riffsland from my childhood, and now when it has become a reality, I have messed up everything. I don't know why I entered into that chamber or why I touched the Blood Shredder, but the only thing I knew was I did not want to leave Riffsland.'

'Sleep well, Jonathan. Mendis will soon arrive to join you in the bed,' Dimitri said and moved on.

'Are you also a legend, Dimitri?' Jonathan shouted as Dimitri had gone far.

'I am a Nimbler, and we are not musicians,' Dimitri said and stepped into the hallway while Jonathan kept looking at the city.

CHAPTER TEN

WARGSKULT

On the next morning, loud sound of drums and horns forced Jonathan to wake up. He found that Mendis was sleeping just beside him. Jonathan got up from bed and stepped towards the balcony and saw that two troops were entering through the marketplace and were being greeted by everyone in the city. There were two different chariots leading the troops. On one chariot, there was a muscular man with cream-colored long hair in sleeveless leather jacket and leather pant. He was having black leather wristband on both of his hand and was looking very rude, while the other one was with a lady who was blonde and in a red gown. The man with the lady was looking just like Thor and his dress was also the same.

'Who's there?' Mendis asked, rubbing his eyes.

'Where have you been? We are not on a picnic trip,' Jonathan shouted on Mendis.

'Look, someone is here,' Mendis said, pointing towards Jonathan's back.

'Get ready, the members of Wargskult are here. Oh, Blake Dyer, Luke Knight with Sarah Knight,' Dimitri said, looking at the troops.

'Who is Blake Dyer, and who is Luke Knight?' Jonathan asked.

'The one alone in the chariot covered in leather from top to bottom is Blake Dyer, and the one with the lady is Luke Knight. Don't worry; you will meet everyone in the meeting.'

Jonathan and Mendis entered into the hall, where they met with The Three in which there was a long dining table in the middle with a number of chairs around it. But this time all the chairs were filled. In front of the table, Valdus, Rother, and Zorich were sitting, while in the right-hand side row, George; Zoran; Margret; Dyer, the drummer of Wargskult; Luke, the rhythm guitarist of Wargskult with his wife, Sarah, were sitting. Just in front of them, a short-heighted guy with black long hair, clean-shaved in a full-sleeved brown V-shaped collar and tight pants, was sitting. Jonathan heard from Sivur about the vocalist of Wargskult and how he looked like and he was sure that this short-heighted guy was Stephen Marflet.

Everyone's eyes turned towards Jonathan, which made him stop on the position he was.

'Keep standing,' Dimitri whispered to Jonathan and stepped towards a vacant chair. He climbed up to the chair and sat upon it.

'Where are Finn and Daniela?' Valdus asked George.

'Sorry for the delay, Sir Valdus. Our troop was attacked by Locus tribes who got the information from black whisperers,' Finn Henwood, the bassist of Wargskult, said, taking a chair out for Daniela Henwood, his wife.

Finn Henwood was having a mustache and was wearing a leather tunic over white shirt. He looked like a gentleman and so was his wife who was in a gown, having brown hair, which was tied beautifully together on the top. She was wearing velvet-colored gloves with diamond bracelets.

'Oh, these black whisperers. They are very irritating,' Dyer said, rapping the table with his hand.

'By the way, who is the one?' Stephen asked suspiciously, looking at Jonathan and Mendis.

Mendis stepped back from where he was standing. Jonathan looked beside him and found that Mendis was standing back.

'He is very small. But I heard that he knows much about Riffsland,' Daniela said.

'Yes, and George is not happy about it,' Margret said.

'I don't care what he knows, the only thing I care about is how he found the Blood Shredder,' George argued.

'You have lots of guts, my child. I can say this for sure that you are having a bright future and you will be a great musician,' Dyer said.

'I am thinking of sending him on the Journey of Last Hope,' Valdus said and everyone went mum.

'What, the Journey of Last Hope? We don't know who this kid is? How he touched the Blood Shredder by crossing the Wall of Bats, Cursed Water, and the Crowned Witch? We can't let the future of Riffsland into the hands of a kid from the other world,' George said furiously.

'So what do you want? We will wait till the Guttadevers find the three powers and attack on our city to take the other instruments?' Luke said.

'But they have not been able to find it till now.'

'But, George, till now, no one was able to break the rock of Blood Shredder, but it has happened. We can't predict the future, but we can control it to some extent by making our present secured,' Rother said politely.

'Sir Rother is right. We should give him a try. If he can get near to Blood Shredder without any training, without any power, then he must be having something special in him,' Stephen suggested.

'I heard that the guard said that he turned the guitar into a hammer. It means he is somehow related to Riffsland. But he is a small kid. We can't put his life in danger,' Sarah, wife of Luke Knight, said.

'I asked Zoran to search about his past when he was in his sleep from the shock of the Blood Shredder and he found nothing,' Zorich said.

'Yes, yes. I looked into his mind. He is the single child of his parents. He is also a lead guitarist of his band. I looked at all of his family, but he has no any relation with Riffsland,' Zoran mumbled.

'And what about that servant from which he has been hearing the stories of Riffsland?' Margret asked.

'His servant has no relation with Riffsland. He is also a simple old man. I think the Gorams living in the ordinary world have spread the secret of Riffsland, and from word of mouth, it has spread from one person to another as a fictional story. The other boy is also a musician. His parents are also musicians but having no relation with Riffsland.'

'He is a freak. He can read minds,' Mendis whispered.

'Shut up,' Jonathan said.

'But the Black Strip of Bond is also lost. We can't say it for sure that the Gorams have spread this secret,' Dyer said.

'By believing on Gorams, we can't decide our next step. They are a bunch of backstabbers, liars, and the worst living creatures on earth,' Stephen said.

'What about the two Gorams who have been captured?' Dyer asked.

'They have sealed their mouth with the Black Mud. Now no one can make them say anything,' Rother said.

'What are your views, Dimitri?' Valdus asked Dimitri who was sitting silently in the hall from the start.

'This boy is faithful, we can believe in him, and regarding the journey, I think this is the right time.'

'That's why I like you, Dmitri, calculated and needed words,' Valdus said and smiled.

'But a boy coming from the other world, with the Gorams, knowing everything about Riffsland, breaking the stone of Blood Shredder, and now we are sending him on the Journey of Last Hope?' George said.

'He is innocent and nothing to do with our world. Why should we put his life in danger?' Sarah argued again.

'But Zoran has already looked into his mind and he is clear. I think the time has come to raise the Blood Shredder again, which we have been trying from so many years,' Daniela said.

'I am also with Daniela,' Finn said.

'I think everyone has agreed to send Jonathan instead of some . . .,' Margret said, stopped, and threw a sharp glare at George.

'We will do what Sir Valdus will say. What's your decision, Sir Valdus?' Finn muttered.

'Jonathan will go on the journey, but only if he wants to,' Valdus said, getting up from his chair.

'Ask this boy,' Zorich said.

'Are you ready to go?' Rother asked softly, putting his hand on Jonathan's shoulder.

Jonathan looked behind and saw Mendis signaling to dissent the proposal.

Jonathan opened his mouth, swallowed, and said, 'Yes.'

'I knew that. This boy is brave,' Dyer babbled, ramming the table again.

Mendis pushed Jonathan as they entered into their room.

'Have you gone mad? You agreed upon going on a journey when we were on the way to home. You have messed up everything, Jonathan,' Mendis squealed.

'I have something because of which I was able to find the Blood Shredder and touched it and now I want to discover it. We will get back to our home, Mendis, and they have not forced us to do this. I agreed upon it,' Jonathan said.

'You have something special, then why am I being dragged into it? I have nothing to do with it,' Mendis growled.

'I think now you are being jealous because I have touched the Blood Shredder and you haven't done anything yet,' Jonathan dinned.

'Oh, that's what you think. Then go on the journey alone and I am not going to join you. Go to hell, Jonathan,' Mendis said hotly and moved towards the balcony.

Jonathan knew that Mendis is doing all this for protecting Jonathan. The journey was full of danger and with chances of not returning back. Mendis was Jonathan's savior from childhood and he was angry because Jonathan was putting his life in danger. Jonathan knew that Mendis thought that if he would not go on the journey, Jonathan will also cancel his plan, but Jonathan knew that Mendis will come back for sure.

On the same night, Sarah with her husband, Luke Knight, came to meet Jonathan.

As usual, Jonathan was standing in the balcony and watching the whole city.

'Hello, Jonathan,' Sarah said.

'Oh, Miss Knight.' Jonathan was surprised to see that the rhythm guitarist of Wargskult and the greatest flamenco player, Sarah, had come personally to meet him.

'Looks like you love the view from here. When Zorich brought me here, I was also of your age and I also used to spend most of my time here,' Luke said.

'Do you used to have these muscles from that time?' Jonathan muttered.

'No, my son, I was very thin then. But time changes everything. I have come here to wish you a safe journey and I am very much happy that you have accepted the proposal of going on to the journey without any greed and relation,' Luke said.

'You are brave, Jonathan. If we would've had a kid, he must have been of your age. Take this, Jonathan. It's a locket of luck which my father gave me. It's been protecting me from my birth and now I want it to be yours,' Sarah said, opening her locket and giving it to Jonathan.

It was a locket on which two fairies were sitting around a throne. It was hexagon in shape and was of gold.

'Thank you, Miss Knight.'

'Where is your friend, Jonathan?' Luke asked, looking here and there.

'Oh, he went with Dimitri to see the kingdom,' Jonathan lied as Mendis, after having an argument, asked Dimitri to shift his room.

'Bye, Jonathan. Have a safe journey. We will be leaving tonight because some problems need to be solved at High Hills. I am sure we will meet again,' Sarah said and kissed Jonathan on his head.

'Bye, son. Be brave and bring back the three powers. We have hopes from you,' Luke said and they both left the balcony.

CHAPTER ELEVEN

WHISPERERS

Next day on the breakfast table, Zoran was licking his bowl of soup when Dimitri said, 'I don't think even a little bit of rivalry between any of the travelers would be good.'

'You are talking about Mendis and Jonathan,' Zoran mumbled, licking the last drop of soup.

'Yes. They both are part of journey, and if this type of relation will go on, the pressure and frustration will swell for sure.'

'So what do you think?'

'Why don't you take both of them to the market? They might realize what is the value of this journey and how many lives are dependent on it,' Dimitri said.

'Yes, yes, good idea, but only after another bowl of soup.'

'Why are we going to the market?' Jonathan asked.

'And especially with him,' Mendis murmured from back.

'I thought some fresh air and new people will make up your minds,' Zoran said, stepping down from the stairs that connected the land from the palace.

Zoran took them to the market, crossing which they reached the kingdom. But things were changed now. Everyone was giving a smile back to Jonathan and Mendis, which was making both of them a little surprised, because this was their second day in Riffsland and how could everyone know them. Suddenly a lady came running from a bakery stall and gave two pieces of chocolate cake to Jonathan and Mendis.

'This is for you, from my side,' the lady said, smiled, and stepped aside.

'Do these people know us?' Jonathan asked Zoran.

'Yes, they know everything and are very much happy about the journey. Because after the journey, they will not have to sleep with the fear of Guttadevers in their heart,' Zoran said, checking a pumpkin on the stall. The pumpkin seller also passed a wide smile to Jonathan and Mendis.

'But how so fast?' Mendis said.

'You heard at the meeting about whisperers who helped in attacking Finn and Daniela? Their ears are very much sensitive and they like spreading the news which they call the whispering.'

'But why did they help in attacking them?' Mendis asked.

'There are some bad whisperers out there. But some are good, faithful, and loyal. These loyal whisperers protect our whispering from being spread into the bad whisperers behind these gates. And they also spread only those messages which we want and in return we give them protection from the bad whisperers.'

'You mean to say, if these whisperers will not be with us, no one would've known anything about us within this kingdom? And why haven't we seen any one of them?' Mendis asked.

'Yes, you are right, and right now he is hiding behind you in the hood.'

As Zoran said, a small white creature jumped off from Mendis who was of nearly one foot with toga wrapped around his body and the white color was looking like plaster paint because it was all over his body. His clothes and eyes were big, but his body's width was similar to his head. He was bald, wearing a small gold finger in right hand, and was looking very scared.

'Offer him some chocolate, that's the only thing they like,' Zoran said.

Mendis took out a piece of cake and offered it to the small whisperer. He leaned to a side behind the wooden stick due to the aroma of chocolate and came slowly towards it. As he took the chocolate, he smiled, shook Mendis's finger, and as Mendis turned, he again got vanished.

'He was very cute,' Jonathan said.

'They don't speak and are master at hiding. The only way to call them is by chocolate. They are very innocent and emotional.'

'If they can't speak, how do they whisper?' Jonathan questioned.

'They don't speak, they just touch their finger on someone's head and it tells them what they have heard, but they can whisper a thing only once, because then they forget what they have heard. But they can't speak. Their technique of touching only copies the thing they hear. But while letting them enter in our city, we agreed upon some terms. Like, they will not whisper anything which will affect the peace and love of Riffsland, they will not whisper someone's good secret to others and interfere in someone's personal matters.'

As Jonathan and Mendis were checking the marketplace, an old lady came from the left.

'Are you the one who is going on the journey?' the old lady asked.

Mendis looked towards Jonathan, swallowed, and then said, 'Yes.'

'Thank you for your effort, you are very brave, and my blessings will always be with you,' the old lady said and they moved on. Mendis was still looking back into the eyes of the old lady, which were full of hope.

Mendis looked at Jonathan who was gaping at him.

'Let's go on the terrace of this building,' Zoran said, pointing towards a building at the right.

The people in the house greeted Zoran as he entered into the house.

'It's our pleasure, Sir Zoran, that you visited this house. Oh, looks like you are with the two brave boys who are going on to the journey. Come back from the journey and we will greet you with our sweet dishes. My wife is a master at it,' the old man said, bowing down in front of them.

'Look, look, Pamela. They are the one,' a small kid whispered to another kid sitting next to him.

'When I grow up, I will also be like them,' another one said.

They went on to the terrace, and as Jonathan looked at the place behind the walls, he was very much surprised.

'How can this be possible? When Sir George and you carried me from the cliff, it was all rocky and barren fields with not even a single tree and now it's a jungle out there.'

'It's another mystery of Riffsland. During day, this place turns into the barren field, and when night spreads it legs, it turns into a jungle. But on the day of full moon and festival, it turns just opposite and the day you came was full moon. It was a curse by a person of Guttadevers army.'

'Who is that?' Mendis questioned.

'It's better if you don't know about him.'

Suddenly Mendis looked at his hand and found that there was a spot of white color from the whisperer who touched his finger.

'Hey, Zoran, look. It looks like the whisperer was not white colored but he has painted himself.'

'Oh that. In actuality, the whisperers are black in color, but when these good whisperers came here, they wanted to differentiate themselves from the bad ones. That's why they painted themselves white and that's the reason they hate rain, because it washes their color. They are a little weak from mind and the golden ring which you saw was to make their own identity because they are similar to each other, and to let other people know, each of them wear different things but a common toga.'

'These people have lots of hope from us,' Mendis said.

'Yes, they have, and they consider both of you very brave,' Zoran said and smiled.

Now Mendis was back to Jonathan's room but still they were not talking to each other. Mendis was still busy in feeding the whisperer who was having a ring.

'Here is the list of persons going on the journey. Sir Valdus has said to distribute it to everyone. Oh, these whisperers are in love with you,' Dimitri said, handing over a piece of paper to Jonathan and looking at Mendis.

'Okay, me, Zoran, you, Mendis, and—' As Jonathan was going to read the other names, Dimitri cut him off.

'Malphus, Zorich's best disciple who knows about the different life-survival techniques outside this world and also about dragons; a whisperer, which is being sent on Mendis's demand; and Theodore, the son of the late Andrew Blake and Isabel Blake.'

'They have a son,' Jonathan said in alarm and jumped off from his bed.

'Yes, he is returning tonight from his tour of Last Fret and I don't think that he is very much happy about the journey and especially with you,' Dimitri said.

'I didn't know that.'

'There are many things in Riffsland which you still don't know. He is very good, but a little upset because the Blood Shredder which belonged to his dad has been touched by a normal boy. Everyone was expecting it to be done by Theodore, but you did it.'

'It means we will have problems on journey.'

'Yes, this is not going to be a vacation,' Dimitri said and left the room.

Jonathan was stunned. He looked at Mendis who was raffling the whisperer. Jonathan slowly stepped towards Mendis and said, 'I am sorry, Mendis. I didn't mean it. I didn't know that you are coming on the journey.'

'It's okay. I was being a little selfish, but this is not your journey now. This is ours,' Mendis said and hugged Jonathan tightly.

'Looks like these whisperers have become your good friend. But why have you recommended them for the journey? And how did they allow them to go with us?'

'It's between me and whisperers. We are very good friends and we never break our secrets. Right, whisperer?' Mendis asked from the whisperer and he nodded his head.

'Okay, okay, I am not going to interrupt you both. But this Theodore doesn't look good and I didn't know that Blake family had a son.'

'I think he has arrived and he must be sprouting the flood of bitter words about you.'

'Hey, can you use this whisperer to hear what Theodore is talking about?'

'No, no. I think you didn't hear what Zoran said about the agreement between these whisperers and them.'

'Please, for once. I am begging you, Mendis.'

'Let me try,' Mendis said and looked towards the whisperer.

He was looking a bit scared and was frightened.

'Don't be scared. This is not breaking up your agreement. You are breaking none of those,' Mendis said and the whisperer got vanished.

'He ran away?' Jonathan asked.

'Yes, towards Theodore's room,' Mendis said and smiled.

After waiting for long in the balcony, they saw the whisperer coming by hiding from one side of the passage to another. He came near Mendis, climbed on him, and touched his head with his finger.

'What, what?' Jonathan asked with curiosity.

'Theodore was complaining to Miss Margret about you. He was asking how everyone can trust a common boy. He doesn't belong to Riffsland and don't need to do a favor on us. Theodore also said that only because Sir Valdus, Rother, and Zorich have agreed upon it, he is ready to go on the journey, but the Blood Shredder belongs to him, and once all the three powers will be brought back, he will raise his guitar and wake up his mom from the twenty years of dead sleep.'

'These whisperers are very much helpful,' Jonathan said.

'And don't dare ask me to do these types of things again. By the way, when are we moving for the journey?' Mendis asked, taking the whisperer down on ground and feeding him with a chocolate.

'Day after tomorrow,' Jonathan said and raffled the whisperer.

CHAPTER TWELVE

FATHER AND BREAKFAST

Jonathan tried, tried, and tried, but was not able to sleep. He closed his eyes, banged his head with the bead four times, and exercised for half an hour but still he could not sleep. He was struggling with his usual problem and he started considering himself as a night hunter.

He saw that the white whisperer was eating the remaining pieces of chocolate on the table. Jonathan got up from his bed and moved towards the table. The whisperer looked towards Jonathan, ignored, and again got busy in eating.

Jonathan took the piece of chocolate from the whisperer. He looked suspiciously towards Jonathan and then made a face that no one can ignore. Jonathan returned back the piece of chocolate to him. All of a sudden, when Jonathan was looking at the bright sky, the whisperer got vanished. Jonathan looked on the table, beneath it, but the whisperer was not there.

As Jonathan stood up, someone poked him from the back. Jonathan turned around, but no one was there.

Again someone poked him and this time Jonathan saw the whisperer hiding behind the bed. Jonathan moved slowly towards the bed, pretending that he doesn't know where the whisperer was, and as he jumped off to grab the whisperer, he snatched the list of travelers given by Dimitri and ran towards the boundary. Jonathan ran behind him.

It was looking like the whisperer was in the mood to play because he could have hid anywhere and Jonathan wouldn't have been able to find him for his entire life, but he was running all across the balcony. Following him from the balcony to the hallway, they now reached near the main gate. The moon was glittering bright and wolves were howling loud. The whisperer was standing in front of the gate and Jonathan stopped panting.

All of a sudden, Sir Zorich appeared in front of the door. Jonathan was stunned. The whisperer ran towards Sir Zorich who took him into his lap and raffled him.

'Not able to sleep?' Zorich asked coldly.

'I was just playing with the whisperer,' Jonathan muttered and the whisperer in the laps of Sir Zorich passed a sharp glare at Jonathan.

'They are very good and can be used for many purposes,' Sir Zorich said.

Jonathan opened his mouth, swallowed, and then said, 'Yes, Sir Zorich.'

'Breaking the rules for the betterment is not against the law. Rother acts as a balance between me and Valdus. He speaks a lot while cooking or making someone eat what he cooks, and Valdus, he believes in the books and anyone in Riffsland is not above than the rules for him.'

'I know, Sir Zorich, and I am sorry for that,' Jonathan apologized.

'You shouldn't be because even I don't believe in following the rules.'

'That's why everybody consults you first for anything, but everyone said you don't speak much.'

'I speak when it's necessary. I was talking to Father. He is very good at suggestion.'

'But I have heard that he talks to few persons only,' Jonathan said, taking the whisperer back from Sir Zorich's lap.

'He talks only to those whom he finds important,' Sir Zorich said and Jonathan looked towards the door.

'Good night, Mr. Jonathan,' Sir Zorich said, striding away.

Jonathan, taking the whisperer into his hand, slowly moved towards the door. He was still thinking how someone can speak so coldly and with a brick's expression. He reached close to the door, touched it with his hand, and whispered, 'Father.'

And when he opened his eyes, he was in a dark jungle and the same tree, which everyone called The Father with face at its trunk, was just in front of him.

'I was expecting you,' Father croaked.

'Hello, Father,' Jonathan muttered.

'So you are going on the journey. One thing I must say that you are very brave, but much more curious.'

'Sir Zorich told me about you. I thought that you only talk to special people.'

'Yes, that's true, and you are very special. Come sit on my root,' Father said and Jonathan moved towards him. He sat slowly on his giant root.

'Do I belong to anyone here? How I got these powers which turned a guitar into a hammer?'

'Time will tell you everything. Playing with it is not a good sign, but one thing is for sure that the time you have thought to spend here in Riffsland is going to be much more than expectation.'

'Dimitri said that Theodore is not happy with me.'

'Oh, Dimitri, he is the best Nimbler I have ever seen,' Father said, ignoring Theodore.

'How these Nimblers came here to work, Father?' Jonathan asked.

'Oh, they used to live up on mountains and had good relation with us. They were the most peace-loving living creatures I know. They lived happily without disturbing anyone. But one day the monsters attacked them because of their enormous source of minerals and other things on their land. They were not warriors, but they fought well with them. But the monsters also took help from the giants of Gorgentus and they won. We from Riffsland send our troops to save them and get their land back. But monsters cursed the land with poison so that it would be neither for them nor for Nimblers. Seeing this, we gave shelter and food to these Nimblers and promised them to feed them for a lifetime. But these Nimblers hate being favored by anyone and consider it as begging, so they work for us in return of which we give them food and shelter. From that day till now, they live in Riffsland and work with Rother to make instruments.'

'They are very good, but I have only met one of them, Dimitri.'

'Yes, they are, and he will be very helpful on the journey which you have bravely decided to go on.'

'Father, I still think whether my decision of going on to the journey is wrong or right. I am putting my friend's life in danger, bringing hopes in eyes which I don't think will be fulfilled. I did it for my own selfishness.'

'Finding what you are is not selfishness. If in your life, if you deserve to be at some better place, where people need you, you must snatch that place and throw away the mask of pretending to be a normal boy. It needs years and years of practice to become a Shredder, but you just touched the guitar and it turned into a hammer. You have something special in you. Have belief in it and on your friend who trusts that power which lives within you. It is the special thing inside you which rose hopes in their eyes, and if you will doubt on yourself, then how will others be able to believe you?'

'Am I really special?'

'Yes, you are, my child. Let the time come and you will realize that this is not just a journey but the beginning of your new life,' Father said and Jonathan hugged a big root coming out from Father.

'Thanks, Father.'

'Oh. From so many years, no one has hugged me,' Father said.

On the next day, Jonathan and Mendis were called by Sir Rother for breakfast, just a day before starting for the journey. They were excited about it because everybody said that Sir Rother is also a great cook. He was considered as the soul of Riffsland, because he was the one who made the instruments for Riffsland. All the instruments in Riffsland, from violins, flutes, guitars, drums, bagpipers to harmonicas, piano, synthesizers, were made by Sir Rother. People said that he loves kids and is very soft-hearted. He gets easily attached with anyone and Nimblers were the best examples. They used to work for him, but Sir Rother considered them none other than his children. Everybody said that on the Darkest Day, he single-handedly fought and injured the one who cursed the forest.

Two small Nimblers were ordered to take Jonathan and Mendis to Sir Rother's room, where the breakfast was planned. The Nimblers were looking very serious and not even talking to each other. Jonathan passed a sharp glance at Mendis, pointing towards the pale-faced Nimblers. They were trying to move fast and match the speed with Jonathan and Mendis but were struggling with their short legs. The door of Sir Rother's room was a piece of artistic marvel. There were countless numbers of instruments drawn on the door.

'It's mesmerizing,' Jonathan drawled.

'Yes, it is,' Mendis supported.

'This door of Sir Rother contains every instrument in the world. No one in the world can make instruments like him,' one of the Nimblers said coldly and another Nimbler slowly opened the door.

It was a big room with a dining table in middle and a set of sofa just behind it. On the wall, as expected, there were many instruments hanging. There was also a poster of Sir Rother with hundreds of Nimblers near the sofa set. The two windows right in front of the main door opened into the spectacular view of sky and the forest.

'Oh, so here you are,' Sir Rother said, coming out of another room in a white apron on which there were spots of chocolate and wheat.

'Hello, Sir Rother, your room is very nice,' Jonathan muttered.

'Oh, thank you. It is all decorated by these Nimblers. They are like my son. Thank you, Zin and Fog, for bringing Jonathan and Mendis here,' Sir Rother said and the two Nimblers moved into the room from which Sir Rother came.

'Come, sit on the table. The breakfast is ready.'

'For sure,' Mendis said and they moved on towards the table.

Sir Rother also joined them on the table while the two Nimblers came with two covered plates in their hands. By stretching their hands to maximum, the Nimblers put the plates onto the table.

'Thank you very much, Zin and Fog. You can also join us, if you want.'

'No, Sir Rother. We have to still complete the four guitars and one harmonica,' one of the Nimblers said.

'As you wish.'

'So this is chocolate cake which is my favorite, this is pie, some salted snacks, and my special coffee. Hope you will like it,' Sir Rother said, opening the covers one by one.

'It smells delicious, Sir Rother,' Jonathan said and Mendis attacked on the food. He shoveled the pie and cake at once.

Seeing his devouring signs, Sir Rother passed on the whole plate towards him. Mendis looked at Sir Rother, smiled with the mouth filled with pie, and then again started eating.

'Don't be shy, Jonathan. You will not get good food on the journey,' Sir Rother said, passing on the piece of chocolate cake from which chocolate syrup was trickling.

'Thank you.'

'They say that the one who cursed the jungle was injured badly by you, single-handedly,' Jonathan babbled, taking the first sip of coffee, the aroma of which was fantastic.

'Yes. I like discussion on a cup of coffee and sometimes even storytelling. His name was the Dark Soul. He was very perilous. Wherever he goes, the dark power follows him like a black cloud hovering all around. It was a very furious battle. My left hand was injured by him and I still have the scars,' Sir Rother said, folding his full-shelved doublet dress from the right hand and showing a black scratch.

'Does it still hurt?' Mendis asked curiously.

'No, no. It doesn't hurt now, but the time when I got it, it was paining so badly that dying was the only option left. Thanks to Valdus and Zorich who threw him away into the other world, means your world, and sealed the door from which you have entered.'

'Did he also attack Riffsland?' Mendis asked.

'Yes, yes. While everyone was engaged in the battle, he somehow managed to sneak and enter in Riffsland. Still no one knows why. He started killing our citizens and everybody says that he was trying to reach near Isabel Blake. But while returning back from Riffsland, he was thrown away through the gate with some other great evil powers which were on the side of Guttadevers.'

'It means he is still alive in the other world. I mean our world,' Jonathan asked.

'Ya, he might be. It's been twenty years since the battle. But still the wounds of the lost one are new. Andrew Blake, Isabel Blake, and many others who lost their lives in the battle,' Sir Rother said glumly.

'Oh, in between our talks, I forgot to show you my factory where instruments are made. Let's go. Follow me,' Sir Rother said, getting up from the table and moving into another room.

Sir Rother opened a gate of a trapdoor into the other room, which was leading through steps. He went under it and Jonathan and Mendis followed him. It was looking like a workshop lighted by lamps, hanging on the wooden pillars, supporting the upper floor. There were hundreds of Nimblers engaged in making instruments. They were working like there is nothing more important for them. Some Nimblers were putting strings on guitar while some were testing the newly made piano with a marvelous finishing. There were woods and woods everywhere. They were being cut off, furnished, polished, and being given the shape of instruments. The Nimblers were looking very skilled in their own particular task and there coordination and synchronization was awe-inspiring.

All the Nimblers were sweating and their clothes were having spots of grease, oil, and many other things, but their dedication was on its verge. Their looks were almost similar to Dimitri.

'Good morning, Sir Rother. Oh, hello, Mr. Jonathan and Mendis. Sir Dimitri always tells us about you,' one of the Nimblers coming from left-hand side, putting his hacksaw blade away, said.

'Yes, yes, Finlet. They are the ones who are going on the journey,' Sir Rother said.

'We wish you best of luck, Mr. Jonathan and Mendis, and welcome you to our factory of instruments which is the birthplace of all the instruments made in Riffsland under the guidance of Sir Rother,' Finlet said.

'Thank you, Finlet,' Jonathan muttered.

'Every child when starts crawling is brought near the revolving symbol of instruments which is called the Faitiny, made from the words *faith* and *destiny*. It contains all the instruments in the world which keeps revolving up and down, side to side. When the child touches the Faitiny, it stops and shows the instruments touched by him and that instrument becomes his destiny, which is made here.'

'Where is the Faitiny?' Jonathan asked.

'Sorry, my child, but I can't show you the Faitiny because it can't be shown to anyone else other than a Riffslandian, and if it is shown to others, a crack will appear in it. One crack has already been made by the Dark Soul. And it takes months to repair a crack, but the crack by Dark Soul has become permanent. He is the most powerful warrior of the Guttadevers and stopping him is almost near to impossible.'

'I wish I never get to meet him,' Jonathan said with bated breath.

CHAPTER THIRTEEN

THE JOURNEY

On the next day, Mendis, Jonathan, Zoran, Dimitri, Malphus, Theodore, and a whisperer were all ready to start the last journey. And for the last time, they were standing before The Three in the hall.

Malphus was of average height with blond hair, which was not tied. His armory was carved with images of dragons and he was not very muscular. He was looking very mysterious with strange things like a bird's skull hanging from his pocket, a blood-colored feather, two dices with six dots on all sides. On the other side, Theodore was having curly and light brown hair, which was long and was suiting well with his shining face. His face was a semblance of pride and rudeness, which was not a good sign for Jonathan and Mendis. Theodore always used to wear a bracelet given by his mother. The bracelet was of silver with the sign of both moon and sun at a mountain.

'The only thing I want from all of you is to return safely from the last journey. Don't take it as a do-or-die situation, it's just an attempt to bring back what we lost twenty years back and to wake a lady who sacrificed everything for Riffsland,' Valdus said.

'We will bring the three powers for sure, Sir Valdus. This time the Blood Shredder will not be in chamber 631 but will be in my hands,' Theodore said.

'Very good, Theodore. An enthusiastic starts leads to a successful end, but don't forget why this journey after so many years is going to start again. You might be the son of the late Andrew Blake, but family brings only glory, it does not bring the talent. You will have to develop it by yourself. And for you two, Jonathan and Mendis, one thing is for sure, that even for the attempt you are making, we will not be able to repay the debt of it,' Rother said.

'This is the drop of life. It contains only one drop which you will have to use wisely. If it will be used properly, it can snatch anyone of you from the hands of death,' Zorich said, handing over a small glass flask to Jonathan.

'We will try our best, sir, and I hope we will fulfill your expectation,' Jonathan said and they moved on.

On the way to the main door of the kingdom, Finn and Daniela Henwood with Margret Blake, George, and Blake Dyer were standing. They all gave their blessing and best wishes to the travelers of the Journey of Last Hope and they stepped on to the long stairs to start their journey by passing through the city. In the city, everyone was standing on both sides of the road to greet them for their journey. Everyone was having a smiling face and were waving goodbye. Kids were running behind them and flowers were being poured from the top of the terraces. This faith and belief on the travelers gave them hope to complete the journey.

The bridge ended and the doors were closed. Now there was no returning back. The only way to return back was by bringing the powers back or coming back with low heads without completing the journey. But for once, they looked at Riffsland and everyone remembered some faces that were still hoping for their return and were counting on them. This enthusiasm helped them to move on in the jungle. They were having the plan to move slowly at daytime and faster at night because at daytime, due to the jungle, it was difficult to move, but at night, when the whole jungle was going to turn into a barren field, it was easy to move. They were on their horses in a row and were moving slowly due to the dense jungle.

Now they were much away from Riffsland, looking back, it was only jungle and jungle. The jungle was dense and only filtered sunrays were falling. Even in the bright sunlight, at some places, it was difficult to see. The ground was very uneven and the mud was very wet, which was making it difficult for the horses to make grip.

'With this speed, we will not be able to reach even after a whole year,' Jonathan shouted from the back.

'He is still thinking that he will get the comfort zone of his home and a speed of lightning on this journey. Such a jerk,' Theodore murmured.

'Patience, Jonathan, patience is the thing of uttermost importance here,' Dimitri said.

'Our horses are exhausted. I can hear them asking for rest,' Malphus said.

'Yes. You are right, Malphus. We will take rest at some plain area,' Dimitri said.

'He is very strange and mysterious,' Mendis whispered to Jonathan.

'Yes. I was also thinking the same. How can he understand what the horses said?' Jonathan replied.

After just a few steps, they found a plain area with enough space for six horses and their riders. They made a temporary camp there and decided to rest till night because their plan was to travel for the whole night. They lit fire in the middle of that plain area, tied their horses, gave them food, and made three pairs of two people each, to rotate their round of guarding so that others can rest. Jonathan was sitting with Dimitri and now it was their turn.

'So where are we going first, for the Pick of Dragon, String of Snakes, or for the Buried Belt?' Jonathan asked.

'You want to know about the plan? Wait a second,' Dimitri said and took a green jelly from his pocket. He put it on the ground and burnt it. The smoke from the jelly was green and it started spreading very fast, but only in a small area around them.

'What is this?' Jonathan asked, closing his nose.

'This is the pulp of cherry trees. Whisperers hate it and is the best way to keep them away from our talks and plans being whispered. And from whisperer, I mean the bad whisperer or black whisperer. They whisper like anything and cause hatred and fight among many.'

'But from whom we are hiding our plans?'

'Anyone who feeds them with the blood of bat becomes their master and they can use them for anything.'

'Okay, so now the plan.'

'We are not going for the pick, belt, or strings. At first we will go to the worst market beyond the walls of Riffsland. It is called the Market of Cheaters. They are the one who make the strings and sell it to us. Every part of the instrument is made in Riffsland instead of the strings. But their market is worst of its kind. They fight, cheat, and do all the bad practices of a market. That's why we never visit those market and we have number of traders who brings strings from the Market of Cheaters and take back jewels. These traders of Riffsland don't climb the mountain. They take the long path which takes three days more to visit the market. Instead of the strings, they also bring needy things for our people. Things which are not available in Riffsland or are better and cheaper than Riffsland.'

'So you mean to say that they will tell us where the String of Snakes is and how long it will take to reach there.'

'Yes. They are the only one who knows. The map to the island of String of Snakes and other powers belongs to them. No one from Riffsland has been able to cross the first power and the String of Snakes is the last one. The map which we will get from them will also tell us the way to other two powers. Because the possession of these powers keeps changing.'

'How far is it from here?'

'That you should ask from Zoran because he used to visit the market when he was a trader of Riffsland,' Dimitri said.

Jonathan looked at Zoran, who was sleeping with Mendis, under the jacket of whom the white whisperer was sleeping and snoring.

'Why does Zoran try to be rough, because I don't think he is like that?' Jonathan asked.

'I think because he wants to goes with his personality. He is very innocent and childish, but he doesn't want others to see it. He is always scared of butterflies,' Dimitri said.

'What, butterflies?' Jonathan asked in surprise.

'Yes. But don't tell him that I told you this.'

'Okay, okay. I will not, but butterflies,' Jonathan said, making ugly expressions.

The dawn was near and everybody was taking rest to prepare for the night. As the sunrays started wrapping its cover, the tress and all the greenery started getting engulfed by the earth. It was looking like the sunrays were carrying away the jungle with itself. The earth started to shake and everybody woke up from their dreams.

'What the hell is going around here?' Jonathan asked.

'The moon is coming and sunrays are leaving the jungle,' Malphus said.

'We should get away from the trees,' Theodore said.

And suddenly Mendis's jacket got hooked with a branch of a tree. He thought it as a common thing and turned around to unhook it. But the shaking started getting heavier and Malphus saw that the sunrays were going to pass away from them and were just thirty feet away from them.

'Get into the middle, get away from the trees,' Dimitri shouted and everyone came into the middle.

'Where is Mendis?' Jonathan asked.

And the white whisperer came running and started pulling Malphus's leg. Malphus looked down and saw that the whisperer was pointing at something. Malphus looked into the direction where the whisperer was pointing at and it was Mendis taking his jacket out with ease.

'Mendis!' Malphus shouted and everyone looked at Mendis.

'What?' Mendis asked, smiled, and looked at the trees being engulfed by the earth with the sunrays. His smile turned into a brick's expression.

He started pulling his jacket forcefully and Malphus ran for him, but as Malphus stepped towards him, he got blown away by a tree, which was going into the earth. The sunrays were just near Mendis and he started screaming. There was no way through which others could help him because they were surrounded by the trees going down. The sunrays passed and the tree started going down, taking Mendis with him. Mendis fell on the ground and got stuck to it. Suddenly the sound of tree being chopped off came and the tree fell on the ground instead of going down.

It was Theodore with his guitar, which was now turned into an axe. Mendis was saved and Jonathan ran behind him.

'Are you all right?' Jonathan asked Mendis.

'Yes,' Mendis panted and looked at Theodore.

'Just turning a guard's guitar into a weapon doesn't make you a Shredder and eligible for the journey,' Theodore said and moved away.

Jonathan glanced at Theodore and picked Mendis up.

'Stand on your own. I will not always be there to save your life,' Theodore said and moved towards his horse.

'Will he ever accept the fact that Jonathan has something in him related to Blood Shredder?' Mendis asked as Theodore left the place with his horse.

'He is being taught from his childhood that Blood Shredder belongs only to him and he is the one who can bring it back and do miracles with it. Now at this age, anybody at his place would have been offended by the fact that somebody else has the powers to control it,' Dimitri said.

'He will understand it soon,' Zoran said.

'Should we move on?' Dimitri asked.

'Only after finishing my loaf of bread,' Zoran said, taking out a big piece of bread from his bag.

CHAPTER FOURTEEN

THE FIRST HURDLE

It was all barren again and the moon was shining bright at night. Till now they were going according to the plan. They were moving faster than day because of somewhat plain field and no dense forest around them. Moonlight was falling on the plain field and was making the mountains look more dangerous. There were huge mountains, and on one of them, Jonathan and Mendis stepped for the first time in Riffsland. In the morning, the jungle was full of dangerous animals, the howling of which could be heard, but they were lucky enough to not face anyone of them at night, the barren field was numb till the possible visibility, and it was looking all safe to move on.

'How much time will it take to cross this mysterious jungle, or I should say barren field?' Mendis asked.

'Don't shout. Hear that,' Malphus said.

'I think we are very much near to the Mountain Diggers,' Zoran said.

'Who are the Mountain Diggers?' Mendis asked.

'They live up on those mountains, yes, the mountains, behind which lies the Market of Cheaters. They dig very complicated burrows or passages from which going in is easy but coming out is not possible. Once you get in, they make sure that you will be killed by setting up traps because they use human bones to build an underground room for their king. They leave the bodies to rot so that taking out bones would become easy for them. Just try not to get into those burrows,' Zoran said, looking up at the mountains.

Mendis gulped and said, 'Is there any other way?'

'The other way will take three days more and we don't have that much time,' Dimitri said and they moved on.

They slowly started moving up on the mountain. There was a steeper path, leading all the way up to the mountain. Zoran was leading the troop as he was very much aware of the Mountain Diggers.

'Look at this burrow, even a bear can be dragged into it,' Mendis said, looking at a burrow on the side of the path.

'You are seeing the first burrow of your life of a Mountain Digger,' Zoran said and Mendis pushed his horse away from the burrow.

As they started climbing up, the number of burrows started increasing. It was looking like those of crocodiles who live in big burrows.

'They are many,' Theodore said, looking at the burrows.

'I heard something whispering,' Mendis said, and the whisperer sitting on his shoulder hid under his jacket.

Everyone stopped at their place. They were now on top of the mountain, which was somewhat plain but with lots of burrows on every side.

There was a sound of something coming out from the burrows very fast. Soon the sound started swelling. Everyone started looking at the burrows, and all of a sudden, Malphus's horse fell on the ground in the way like someone had rammed him hardly. Malphus was now on the ground and he took out his violin from the back, which turned into a mace.

'Maplhus, get onto your horse, fast!' Zoran shouted, and as Maplhus ran towards his horse and jumped to sit on it, again something like a black shadow rammed him hard due to which he got banged by a rock and fell unconscious on the ground.

Jonathan jumped from his horse and ran towards Maplhus.

'No, Jonathan, get back to your horse,' Dimitri shouted, but it was too late.

As Jonathan reached near Malphus, a black creature, with skinned body, a tail at the back, two small hands at the front, whole body lying on the ground, and a face of somewhat like an owl with bigger eyes but teeth like crocodile, came from one of the burrow near Maplhus and screeched. It was the Mountain Digger. Jonathan fell on the ground and the Mountain Digger ran towards him with his two hands running on ground like a turbo machine, which was pulling his whole lying body.

As the Mountain Digger came closer to Jonathan, an arrow from the air like a bolt in blue came and hit into the head of the Mountain Digger and white blood sprout out of it. Jonathan looked back; the arrow was from the bow of Zoran. Now everyone was on the ground and with their weapons except for Mendis. He was bare-handed. Zoran was standing with his bow and arrow, which turned from a synth, Theodore was with his axe, and Dimitri was with his hammer. Dimitri passed a small knife to Mendis.

'Take this, kid.'

Mendis caught the knife and looked at its size.

Jonathan stood up and ran towards Malphus. He was still unconscious, so Jonathan dragged him in the middle where all the travelers of the journey were standing.

'Why can't we get back on our horses?' Theodore asked.

'If we will get back on horses, we will be saved, but our horses will be killed or injured like that of Malphus. And without these horses, reaching Cheater's market is not possible,' Dimitri said.

They were standing in a circle and Malphus was waking up in the middle from his unconsciousness.

'Are you all right?' Jonathan asked.

'Yes.'

Suddenly, from one of the burrows, a Digger jumped up like fired ammo from a pistol, but Dimitri's stimulus was much faster than the ammo and he banged the Digger coming towards him with his hammer.

'That was really fast,' Mendis said with shock.

Again a Digger jumped off from a burrow, but when Jonathan tried to move away, another Digger from a burrow, at the back of him, came and banged Jonathan hardly due to which he rolled down on the ground and reached near one of the burrows.

'Move away from the burrow!' Zoran squealed, but it was too late.

A Digger came from the burrow and dragged Jonathan into one of those burrows.

'Jonathan!' Mendis squealed and ran towards that burrow.

'Mendis, no!' Dimitri shouted and Mendis also got rammed and dragged into one of those burrows.

Now because of the distraction from Jonathan and Mendis, the Diggers got a golden opportunity and dragged Theodore and Maplhus too into their burrows.

Dimitri and Zoran were still on the top and were hitting as many Diggers as they could, which were one by one jumping off from their burrows.

Under those burrows, Jonathan fell on the side of a passage from where two ways were leading, one on the right and one on the left. Darkness was more than expected in those burrows. On the other side, Theodore kept slipping into a down-going passage and suddenly he fell into a pit but got hung by a hook. He looked down to see what was in the pit. There were long pointed thorns on which numbers of skulls were lying. Mendis found himself in a small pond in which he fell directly from the burrow. It was all dark there, but he felt that he was not alone there, and suddenly his feeling transformed into reality when he saw a Digger at the top of that pit in the hole from where he fell. He saw Mendis and started laughing like a devil. Mendis knew that it was going to be something very nasty. Mendis started to climb the walls, but it was very much slippery, and suddenly the Digger came crawling on the wall like a lizard. Mendis shrank himself to the corner of the wall, away from the Digger. He came down, looked at Mendis, and took a piece of cloth from his back. He dipped that cloth in the water and again ran on the top. Mendis was confused by the Digger's actions. The Digger took the wet cloth and rubbed it on the wall, and flames came out of it. Now everything was clear and more frightening to Mendis. The water was inflammable and it burnt when rubbed with rock. The Digger started juggling the burning cloth in his hand. Mendis while being stuck to the wall felt that a piece of rock was loose enough to be taken out. He took the piece of rock and kept it behind. As the Digger threw the burning wet cloth, Mendis took out the piece of rock and hit it back towards the Digger. Mendis was lucky. It went directly into the hole and banged the Digger. The Digger suddenly became a live burning Digger. He started screaming and ran away from there.

On the other side, when Jonathan chose to move onto the right-hand side path, he heard something coming very fast, rolling down towards him. The sound was getting louder and closer. Suddenly he saw a big piece of rock coming towards him that was needled. Jonathan started running like anything and the big piece of rock was just behind him. He saw an opening of the passage and ran towards it. But as he reached near the opening, he found that it was a bad decision. It was a dead end with endless depth and the rolling stone was just behind him. Jonathan stepped onto the edge and he saw a bulging piece of rock above the hole, which was enough to climb. The stone was near, but Jonathan grabbed that bulging piece of rock and tried to push himself upward. His legs were still at the hole, and as he again pushed himself upwards, his legs tangled in a hole and he lost his grip. He fell and got hung by his leg upside down and the rock came from the hole like a piston and fell into the endless-looking depth.

On the other side, Theodore's cloth started to tear because of his weight. He started looking for a way to hook up, but the threads of cloth started flicking away, and as he lost the hook and started falling into the bed of thorn, someone grabbed him from the top. It was Malphus.

Mendis on the other side was still in the small pond, and from the hole again, four Diggers came very fast. They were looking very angry and were looking to finish

Mendis as soon as possible, but all of a sudden, they all four fell into the pond like someone has banged them from back. And out of the blue, Maplhus and Theodore came. They took Mendis out of the hole with the help of Maplhus's long mace. Theodore, Mendis, and Malphus were looking for the way out but were reaching the same place again and again.

'This is the same place, look at this carved sign,' Theodore dinned.

'Your cloth smells like the Pink Water,' Maplhus said, coming closer to Mendis.

'Pink Water? It is the water in which I felt.'

'Tear a piece of your cloth and give it to me,' Maplhus said.

'Why?'

'Just give it to me.'

Mendis tore a piece of cloth from his dress and gave it to Malphus. Maplhus took the piece of cloth and put his mace aside.He rubbed the wet cloth on the rock and it started burning. The flame of burning cloth was going in the left direction.

'Our way out is in the left,' Maplhus said and moved on. Mendis and Theodore followed him.

'Yes, this is the way, this is the way!' Mendis shouted with joy as he saw stars from one of the passages.

They slowly crawled to the top, and as they reached near it, the tip of a sword came and stopped just near to the eyes of Mendis.

'Oh! You. I thought the Diggers were coming,' Zoran said and took his sword back.

He gave hand to pull them off out of the burrow. As they came out of the burrow, they saw a bed of dead Diggers on the ground.

'Where is Jonathan?' Dimitri asked, putting his hammer on the back.

'Mendis!' someone shouted from the left-hand side of the mountains.

'It's Jonathan,' Mendis said and they ran towards the left side. Jonathan was hanging upside down, with his legs in the hole.

'My brain is pumping. Pull me up,' Jonathan said after looking at them.

CHAPTER FIFTEEN

CARDS AND CHEATERS

After crossing the Mountain of Diggers, they climbed all the way up to the mountain with their horses. At the top of the mountain, the speed of cold breeze was at its peak. From the top of the mountain, some lights could be seen, which was the Market of Cheaters from where the travelers could get information about the String of Snakes and other powers.

'That is the Market of Cheaters,' Zoran said, looking at the lights.

'It's looking very bright from here,' Mendis said.

'Yes, they don't like darkness and they love anything for exchange which is more beneficial for them,' Zoran said.

'It means to get the information of String of Snakes and other powers, we will also have to suffer a loss?' Theodore asked.

'No, no one has ever been able to cheat them because they are the master in cheating and business. They sell everything, from horses to clothes and also humans. This is the only market which doesn't belong to any part. They have their own world from where anyone can buy. They only accept those deals which is partially beneficial for them. In exchange, they can take anything. And anything means anything, even humans and food. I am a very tough man, but even sometimes I get scared because of them,' Zoran said.

'I am very good at bargaining. Even better than my mom,' Mendis said.

'This is not a vegetable market, my child. In those markets, if you suffer a loss, it would be only in terms of money, but here, life is also at stake,' Zoran said and they started going all the way down to the mountain.

On the way down to the mountain, from very far, the sound of waterfall started coming. When Jonathan leaned down to look where the water was, he saw that the water was coming from the mountain itself and it was leading down the mountain to the place from where light was coming, which according to Zoran was the Market of Cheaters. With the decreasing height of the mountain, the wideness and flow of that water was increasing. While going down on the path, there came a point from where water was falling with huge force, just three feet away from their path. It was so near that one could touch it, but seeing the gigantic waterfall, it was not a good idea.

'This is called as the Source of Life. The water originates from the mountain, which is still a mystery and leads to the big river which is called as the Pearl of Life. It is the same river on which the market of cheaters is based and it will also lead us to the place of Buried Belt,' Dimitri said, touching the water.

They were now in front of the Market of Cheaters. It was a market based on the Pearl of Life, as told by Dimitri. In the middle, there was a water passage for boats, and on both side of the water passage, the market was located. It was well-lighted by lamps and the Cheaters were standing on their different floating shops. The Cheaters were weird. They were skinny, green-colored, with a long tail on their head, and their eyes were of oval shape. They were nearly four feet and were wearing a crossed piece of cloth on top and a wrapped cloth on their legs. Their face was fitting exactly to their name, Cheaters. The items being sold on all the boats varied widely. There were clothes, weapons, jewelry, food, and some human prisoners also. But one thing was same on all the boats; everyone was fighting, bargaining, and shouting on the boats for items being sold. To purchase those items, early men, people from Riffsland, and others were fighting.

'This is the Market of Cheaters. Our traders and other people visit here to buy items. After this market, the place where strings are made is located. We will cross this market, and then after crossing the string's factory, we will visit the head of Cheaters,' Zoran said, looking at a big chocolate cake being sold on one of the shops.

As they were standing, a boat with a Cheater on it came slowly towards them.

'Where would you like to go, sir?' the Cheater asked.

'To the head,' Zoran asked.

'What best you can give for it?'

'Three gold coins,' Dimitri said.

'That will be too less for the long trip.'

'Five gold coins and no more,' Zoran said.

'I like that armory,' the Cheater said, pointing towards Malphus.

'I am not going to give it!' Maplhus squealed.

'Looks like you don't know who we are,' Theodore said.

'Looks like you know how to swim,' the Cheater said and started moving his boat.

'Stop, stop. I am giving it,' Maplhus said.

'Now this is called a good deal.'

Maplhus took out his armory and handed it over to the Cheater with five gold coins. He pushed his boat towards the shore so that they can sit on it. Everyone got onto the boat and the Cheater started moving his boat towards the path.

'This is a wrong deal. I could have set him up in three gold coins,' Mendis whispered to Jonathan.

'They are the best Cheaters out here. Didn't you look into his eyes? He looks like a Cheater from childhood and not only him but everyone,' Jonathan said.

'But I am the king of bargaining,' Mendis said, but Jonathan didn't reply.

Along the path, everyone was just looking at the most weird market they had ever seen. The boat was drafting slowly and the still water was looking very deep.

'These are the worst kind of living creatures I have ever seen. They have no manners, way of living, and they are worthy of their name,' Theodore said and threw a sharp glare at the Cheater moving their boat.

On the still boats, people from Riffsland, who were called as the traders, were arguing, bargaining for items. Instead of the traders, there were other people as well, the dress of whom was looking like that of early men. A big board was also hanging on which there was a list of items being sold in the market and at last it was written, *A gift of white whisperer or any Riffslandn instrument and we will pay you back with a gift of any animal of your demand.*

Instead of that, there were other offers, most of which were partially beneficial to the Cheaters.

'Who are they?' Jonathan asked.

'They are the tribes who live outside the walls of Riffsland because they were not ready to live within the rules of our kingdom. But they are peace-loving, so they established their tribes outside our walls and live peacefully there. We don't interrupt them, neither do they interrupt us. But everyone says that they are very warm-blooded and always ready to kill who betrays them. But not every one of them is good. You heard how they attacked with the help of black whisperers,' Dimitri said.

'How many are they?' Mendis asked.

'There are many tribes outside the walls of Riffsland who are good and many are worst of their kind,' Zoran said and the boat touched the other shore.

They jumped off from the boat and moved towards a big iron gate that was being guarded by two bald giants. As they saw them coming, they opened the gate for them. They were now into the factory of strings. It was a big factory with metals being melted, molded. A number of Cheaters were involved in the process of making the strings and lots of noise was coming out from it. This was the place from where the Cheaters used to make string and traded it to Riffsland. The only reason why they built these strings was the material used to make the strings came under their part of the market and they were also masters at making strings. Many finished strings that were looking awesome were hanging on ropes in series. They were shining like bright silver even at night with low light.

After passing through the factory of strings, they entered into a room where their meeting with the head of Cheaters was decided. The room was made of wood and was very small. Dimitri, Zoran, Theodore, and Jonathan were sitting on the chair while Malphus and Mendis were still standing by their side.

Suddenly a Cheater entered into the room with golden crown on his head, which was slipping off because of its bigger size. He was wearing a blue cape on his back and was looking full of pride. Two small Cheaters entered into the room, following the crowned Cheater.

'I am the head of Cheaters, Mole. Oh, look who has arrived. Theodore Blake, the son of the great Andrew Blake,' Mole said.

'My father's name doesn't suit on your tongue,' Theodore thundered.

'Same anger, it is from your father. Oh, Dimitri, after such a long time, and, Zoran, you have forgotten us after becoming a legend,' Mole sneered.

'We are not here for discussion, Mole,' Dimitri said.

'Neither am I, but these two unknown gentlemen are stinking like the odor of unknowingness.' Mole sniffed.

Mendis stepped backwards as Mole came closer to him and he hid the whisperer into his jacket.

'Whoever you are, bringing a white whisperer is not good because there are too many black whisperers out here, ready to kill him,' Mole said.

The whisperer in Mendis's jacket shrunk himself due to fear.

'We want the information about the three powers of the Blood Shredder,' Dimitri said.

'Oh! A journey again?! Why are you Riffslandians so much eager to sell your life at such a cheap price,' Mole said.

'It's none of your business, we want the information and you will give it to us,' Theodore said.

'You look like a semblance of your father. He was a great man,' Mole said.

'Information about the three powers,' Zoran dinned.

'And what in return?' Mole asked.

'Fifty gold coins,' Zoran said.

'Huh! Gold coins?! It is the oldest way of trading and the information about the three powers which is stored in the Red Paper is a much bigger deal,' Mole said.

'We will give only gold coins.' Zoran strengthened his voice.

'How have you come here?' Mole said.

'By crossing the Mountain of Diggers on our horses,' Dimitri said.

'Six men, it means six horses. No one can pass the Market of Cheaters with their own horses. Either you buy them from here or go all alone. Three horses for the Red Paper, and for other three, I can give you something else,' Mole said.

'Our horses?! No chance. We are not going to give our horses to you, and since when did it become a rule that no one will cross this market on their own horses?' Theodore squealed.

'Just now! Give the horses or go back to Riffsland. At least your life would be saved.' Mole laughed.

'Demand any other thing and we will give it to you,' Dimitri said.

'No, no. I don't want anything else, just the horses. You can pass your time here by paying a horse to play cards,' Mole said.

'Are you sick? We are on a journey and you are talking about playing cards?' Theodore groaned.

'Three horses for the information, one for the game of cards, and I will keep two for bidding,' Mendis said.

'Who the hell are you to interrupt between us?' Theodore growled.

'Same question to you, Mr. Theodore. This boy is fantastic. Deal is done. Which game do you want to play?' Mole asked.

'No, no. This is not the deal. Are you insane, Mendis, Cheaters are the master in card games. You will not be able to win,' Zoran whispered with anger.

'I asked which game, and you know, Dimitri, the rules of Cheaters. Once the deal is done, no one can change it,' Mole said.

'This is the end of the journey,' Theodore said glumly.

'Twenty-nine.'

'Oh, the great game which has originated from the outer world in which the decreasing order of points are jack, nine, ten, spade, king, queen, eight, and seven.'

'Yes, it was originated in India.'

'It doesn't even matter because it's one of my favorites. Take this boy to another room and wait there until I call you back for the game. I always take some time in planning,' Mole ordered and moved on with two small Cheaters. And another Cheater entered into the room to take Mendis with him.

Everyone was paralyzed with what just happened. Now their journey was based upon a game of cards called 29. Everyone was angry, but Theodore was more than angry.

'I knew that bringing these kids will be a headache and they are of no use. The only thing they can do is create trouble,' Theodore growled, but Jonathan didn't reply because he knew this time it was Mendis's mistake.

The other room was all vacant instead of a single chair on which Mendis was sitting with the whisperer moving here and there around the room. Mendis was nervous and was thinking about the game. Someone passed by the door saying, 'The black whisperers are demanding too much to protect everybody's whispering till the white whisperer is here. Sir Mole has paid them only to protect his whispering.'

Mendis looked at the white whisperer who was now sitting in the corner and looking at the room. Mendis called him and he ran towards him. Mendis said, 'I know that this is risky, but we will have to do it. If you can go out and tell me the whispering by the person near to Mole without getting into the hands of black whisperer, then we will get to know about the planning of Mole, because he is a Cheater and there is no doubt that he will cheat in the game.'

Whisperer nodded his head.

'But Mole has paid the black whisperers with the blood of bats to protect his whispering only and sometimes too much cleverness leads to big fall.'

Whisperer was still nodding his head.

'Be careful and come soon. You are my best friend here and I don't wanna lose you,' Mendis muttered.

Whisperer ran towards the corner of the room and mimicked holding a guitar and falling away.

'Yes, yes, you are my best friend, not Jonathan,' Mendis said and the whisperer hugged Mendis's leg and ran towards the door. He jumped off onto it and passed through the window.

After a while, the whisperer came back into the room. He was trying to get into the window, when he suddenly fell off from it but managed to land safely on his feet. He came running towards Mendis and touched his head with his finger.

'Oh, this is their plan, so we can do just opposite of it,' Mendis mumbled.

'Do you have the white color from which you paint yourself?' Mendis asked from the whisperer and he nodded his head.

After half an hour, the small Cheater entered into the room with Mole.

'Looks like you are ready with your plan,' Mole said, taking Mendis away from the white whisperer who was sitting on the chair.

161

While Mole was talking to Mendis, one of the small Cheaters who came with Mole took the white whisperer into his bag and put another whisperer who was also painted white.

'So best of luck for your game, which is already one-sided,' Mole said to Mendis, tapped his shoulder, and moved out of the room, pushing the small Cheater with him who was carrying the white whisperer in the bag and exchanged him with a black whisperer who was painted white.

Mendis looked at the whisperer and he ran towards him. Mendis took him into his hands and looked at it.

The game was being started. Behind Mendis, Theodore, Dimitri, Zoran, and Malphus were sitting and were feeling helpless. Theodore was looking very angry and was thinking how to punish Mendis after losing the game and being the reason of the end of the journey. The game of 29 consisted of four players, two of them were partners. Mendis's partner was Jonathan and Mole's partner was another Cheater.

'Since you have only two horses, we will play two sets. One set for each horse,' Mole said and looked at the whisperer sitting on Mendis's neck.

The game started and Mole distributed four cards to each one. Mendis made the bid and set the color. Mole distributed another four cards and the game begun.

Whenever Mendis was getting the cards, the whisperer was doing the same thing. He appeared on Mendis's neck and then used to hide somewhere. Mendis was winning continuously and Mole was getting frustrated.

'No . . . no . . . no. Not again!' Mole growled as he lost another set.

'Distribute the cards, Mr. Mole, I thought you were a master at cards,' Mendis sneered.

'No talking, just play the cards,' Mole snarled.

And finally Mendis won the first set.

'One horse, Mr. Mole,' Mendis smiled.

'Something is not going right. I can't lose the game,' Mole groaned.

'Yeah, boy. You did it. One more set and we will go with four horses,' Zoran said in joy.

'Four? No, Zoran. Six. Just wait and watch,' Mendis said and continued the game.

Next round started and the same thing started happening again. Every set was being won by Mendis, and Mole was on his peak, but the whisperer was doing the same thing again and again, but with the loss, he was also looking very angry.

But after two games, Mole's luck hit bull's-eye. He started winning. Luck was looking like on his side now. He was bidding for the score and winning the same.

Now both Mendis and Mole were one hand away from winning the set. Cards were distributed and the game started. This time, Mendis bided for it and set the color. He made the bid of 21 and was just 4 points away from it. Mendis threw the card, it was jack of spades, cheater threw 8 of spades, Jonathan threw 9 of spades, but Mole asked for a color and he turned the card. The color was of spades and Jonathan jumped off from the table shouting, 'We won, we won the game!'

Mendis was smiling and looking at Mole who was stunned. Everyone sitting behind Mendis jumped off from their feet and grabbed Mendis in excitement.

'You are the master of cards, Mendis!' Zoran exclaimed, hugging Mendis.

But Theodore was not happy and was just sitting at his place.

'Now we can go with four horses,' Dimitri said.

'Wait a minute, Dimitri,' Mendis said and held the white whisperer sitting on his neck and threw water from his pouch.

His white color started falling with water and the true color of his body appeared, which was all black.

'A black whisperer?! Where is our white whisperer? The paint used by the white whisperers can't be washed with any liquid instead of the rain itself,' Zoran growled.

'Mr. Mole planned to kidnap my white whisperer, in the return of which, group of these black whisperers were ready to work for him for lifetime and they also promised to paint themselves white and tell them my cards so that he can win every set,' Mendis said.

'Where is our white whisperer, and how dare you to touch him?' Theodore said, taking out his guitar, which turned into an axe and put it on Mole's neck.

'It was their plan. The black whisperers, but I swear that they didn't tell me the cards, they are of no use!' Mole howled.

'One more deal, Mr. Mole,' Mendis said.

'Which deal? We have won our horses, we will take back our whisperer and move out from here,' Theodore thundered, pinching the point of axe at Mole's neck.

'You can keep the whisperer which you have kidnapped with you, and in return of which you will get a lifetime service of these black whisperers, but in exchange, I want two horses,' Mendis said.

'Done, done. The deal is done,' Mole said, pushing the axe away.

'You have gone mad!' Theodore growled and rammed Mendis on the wall.

'Now you can't do anything. If a deal is done in Cheater's market, no one can change it.' Mole laughed.

'What are you thinking about? These white whisperers are in our service from past so many years. We promised their protection and now we will use them as items to exchange horses. You can't do this,' Zoran squealed, glaring at Mendis who was hanging on the wall due to the axe on his neck.

Mendis opened his jacket a little bit and signaled Dimitri to look at it. Dimitri came closer to Mendis and looked at his jacket. He again looked at Mendis and said, 'Leave him, Theodore, the deal is done.'

'What? But . . .,' Theodore squealed.

'I said leave him,' Dimitri growled.

Theodore released the pressure and Mendis fell on the ground and started panting.

'A white whisperer in return of just two horses, it is the deal of my lifetime.' Mole laughed and ordered the small Cheater to give them their four horses, two of which they won and two in exchange of the white whisperer and the rest of the two were already with Mendis who kept them for bidding.

They were on the boat and everyone was looking disappointed with the loss of their whisperer. But Mendis and Dimitri were looking very relaxed.

'What, what will we answer to the other whisperers? This is the first time when Riffsland is not able to keep its words,' Zoran said glumly.

Their six horses were on the shore. They moved out of the boat and took their horses.

'Now you can tell them, Mendis. We are away from the market,' Dimitri said, smiling at Mendis and Mendis opened his jacket out of which the white whisperer came and everyone got stunned.

'He is here, then who was the one that got kidnapped?' Malphus asked.

'When I was in the room, I sent my whisperer to get some information from them because I heard that Mole was paying the bat's blood to black whisperers only to protect his whispering and others were unprotected. My whisperer came with the news that Mole has planned to take him away and put a black whisperer in his place, which will help him cheat in the game of cards. But when I heard of this, I caught a black whisperer which was not very easy, and once we got him, we painted him white and put him in our white whisperer's place and hid my whisperer in the jacket. When Mole came to take away the whisperer, he actually took a black whisperer painted white. It was our luck that he didn't show the kidnapped whisperer to the black whisperer or they would have recognized him. Now since the white whisperer was in my jacket, the black whisperer who was painted white was not able to cheat.'

'You mean to say that the whisperer which they have kidnapped is a black whisperer?' Zoran asked.

'Yes. Sometimes too much of cleverness kills your planning,' Mendis said and ruffled the white whisperer sitting on his arm.

On the other side, Mole entered into the room in which the white-painted whisperer was kept with five black whisperers.

'So this is your reward. Now you will work for me for a lifetime,' Mole said

The black whisperers went near the white-painted whisperer and started growling with anger.

'Now what, punish him or kill him,' Mole said.

And then a black whisperer ran toward the bucket kept below a hole in the ceiling that was full of rainwater and poured the water on the white-painted whisperer.

'No!' Mole growled.

CHAPTER SIXTEEN

THE HIDDEN PAIN

They had now crossed the cursed jungle, Mountain of Diggers, and the Market of Cheaters. Their next destination was the Buried Belt, which Dimitri said could be reached by following the river. They were filled with enthusiasm, and Mendis could be credited for it, although Theodore was the unhappiest one because he didn't consider Jonathan and Mendis worthy enough to come on the journey, but Mendis was the reason they were able to protect their whispering throughout the journey and get the information about the three powers that was rolled in a piece of paper given by Mole. The piece of paper was being carried by Malphus in his pocket. It was the Red Paper.

'If we will keep following the river, we will reach the place of Buried Belt. I have checked the Red Paper,' Dimitri said.

'The place where this Buried Belt is situated is also full of Cheaters type of living beings?' Mendis whispered, coming closer to Malphus.

'They are fighters,' Malphus said and Mendis moved away from him with a paralyzed face.

They were going along the river around which there was a jungle but not the cursed one. Since they were following the river, their path was full of obstacles. Sometimes they faced high mountains, which were impossible to climb, and they had to change their path by going around the mountain. It was consuming too much time for them.

'We will rest for the night and will move on in the morning again. The horses have been moving continuously and they need rest,' Dimitri said.

Everyone got off from their horse. Some took out water bags, some went near the cliff, and some were ruffling their horses.

'What's written in the paper? Where is the String of Snakes?' Jonathan asked Malphus who was enjoying the view of the river from the cliff.

'It can't be read normally. This is the Red Paper. It can only be read by pouring someone's blood. And when someone pours his blood on it, it becomes visible only for a minute. So it means every time you need to read it, you must pour your blood, and I think Dimitri has already read it.'

'This is weird,' Jonathan said.

'Nothing is weird; it's all about how you look at it.'

'What are you doing with these stones?' Jonathan asked, looking at three small pieces of stones placed in a row and lines were drawn near them with red chalk.

'Was just checking when my day will come,' Malphus said, putting another stone in the row.

'Is this some kind of magic?'

'No, just a distraction because I was waiting for this journey from long and I knew that one day I will go on the journey and complete what was left long ago,' Malphus said.

'Yes, to complete the Blood Shredder.'

'Everything is not what it looks like,' Malphus said.

'When was the last time you answered anything which will not make you more mysterious?' Jonathan miffed.

'Everyone has some thoughts about what they need to do in their life. The only difference is that some people like to speak loud about it and some keep it within themselves and let others see when it is done.'

'I will never be able to understand you at once, Malphus.'

'And I don't want you to.'

At night, Jonathan was not able to sleep when Theodore was guarding the bonfire alone. As Jonathan's eyes started to blur, a sound of sneaking woke him up. Jonathan moved towards the bonfire and saw that Theodore was not there. The sound of sneaking was coming from the jungle, so Jonathan moved towards it. After moving some distance in the jungle, Jonathan saw that Theodore was sitting near a tree and was sharpening his small sword. Jonathan hid behind a tree to see what Theodore was doing.

As Theodore found that the knife was sharp enough, he made a deep cut on his hand, which made him bleed. Jonathan was surprised to see this all, and when Jonathan's eyes saw the Red Paper, all his doubt got cleared.

Theodore let the blood fall on to the piece of paper, and Jonathan came near him.

'You are still awake. You shouldn't be here. It's none of your business,' Theodore sneered, looking at Jonathan who was standing in front of him.

'Why didn't you do it in the morning?'

'It can only be done in the bright moonlight. And I wanted to do it myself, so I took it from Malphus.'

'What's written in it?'

'The map of the three powers,' Theodore said, looking at the Red Paper.

'Is it far from here?'

'I don't know, it's a difficult map to read, and why the hell am I telling it to you. Your job is to help me bring the

Blood Shredder back with the three powers,' Theodore shrilled.

Suddenly a sound of rushing came into the jungle.

'Who's there?' Theodore shouted.

'Someone is trying to hide,' Jonathan whispered, moving towards the jungle and taking out his small knife.

Theodore also kept the paper in his pocket and took out his guitar, which turned into an axe. They slowly started moving towards the jungle when someone rushed again.

'On the left,' Jonathan said.

The sound of rushing swelled and a large giant, in the dark jungle, jumped off from the bushes towards them. Neither his face nor his body was visible due to the darkness. Theodore and Jonathan dodged the giant and again he vanished into the bushes.

'What was that?' Jonathan screamed.

'I don't know.'

Jonathan crawled towards Theodore who was sneaking towards the sound of rushing.

'Hsshhh, he is near,' Theodore whispered, positioning his axe.

All of a sudden, Jonathan started getting dragged behind by someone. Jonathan squealed and Theodore ran towards him. Jonathan held the trunk of a tree but started losing his grip due to the huge force, which was pulling him.

As Theodore came near to Jonathan, the one holding Jonathan's leg vanished and, like a bolt from blue, banged Theodore from behind. Theodore fell on the ground and now the giant was visible in the bright moonlight. He was long with masculine body, big green eye without any eyebrows, and his mouth looked like it was stitched together and was gray in color. He screamed loudly in the jungle, which went far. Theodore controlled himself and ran towards the giant without any fear. The giant was standing and just looking at Theodore who was running towards him aggressively.

As Theodore jumped to hit him, the giant knocked him with his hand, but Theodore held his hand and poked in his eyes with his axe. The giant got distracted and Theodore jumped off from his hand. But this didn't work, the giant was now much angrier and pulled a big trunk of tree out of the ground and threw it towards Theodore. Theodore dodged the trunk, but it hit Jonathan and he rolled down on the ground. As Theodore looked towards Jonathan, he also got stuck to a tree due to the hands of the giant, pushing him deep inside the trunk. The pressure was increasing and now it was even difficult to breathe for Theodore when suddenly someone hit the giant heavily from the back. The giant left Theodore, who fell on the ground and looked behind.

It was Dimitri with Malphus, Zoran, and Mendis. Mendis ran towards Jonathan and started dragging him aside.

The giant looked at all three of them and howled. Zoran one by one started firing his arrows at the giant, which were giving him shocks because of the current produced by his arrows, while Dimitri and Malphus ran on the opposite side.

The giant was not able to move a single inch due to the raining of electric arrows at him, which were sharp enough to enter an inch into his rocky body. The giant was protecting his face by one hand and was trying to move forward when suddenly Dimitri from behind banged the giant, and as the giant moved towards him, Malphus rapped him again from the other side. The giant got confused and ran towards the other side, seeing which Dimitri, after rotating his hammer for a while, threw it like a pistol that rammed the running giant and he fell on the ground like a dead body, the sound of which went far into the jungle.

Malphus slowly moved towards the lying giant to check whether he is alive or not. He went near the mouth of the giant that was wide open. As he kneeled down to check whether he was breathing, the giant screamed like anything, and Malphus got thrown away. But a sharp shot right into the head of the giant fired by Zoran made him sleep forever.

'What the hell were you two doing here?' Zoran thundered.

'I was reading the Red Paper,' Theodore said ruefully.

'And you?' Dimitri questioned Jonathan.

'I came here following him.'

'He was the giant of Gorgothon, the place where the Buried Belt is located. He could have killed you both or would have ran back towards his village and called others for help. This journey is not only about courage, sometimes you also need to use your mind,' Dimitri said coldly.

'I am sorry. It was my fault. I shouldn't have come here,' Theodore confessed.

'Get back to the bonfire, I will give the guarding now after which Mendis will and hand over the Red Paper,' Dimitri said.

It was morning when Mendis's eyes were trying to shut and were dark red. His whisperer was feeling very cozy in the jacket and was sleeping comfortably. The cold breeze in the morning was forcing Mendis to sleep when suddenly Malphus shook him and asked, 'Where is Theodore?'

'Aaah . . . Theodore . . . yes, yes,' Mendis said sleepily.

'Get up!' Dimitri shouted and slapped him hard on his white cheek, the sound of which shook every part of Mendis's ears and he stood up in shock.

'I don't know,' Mendis mumbled and saw Malphus and Dimitri standing in front of him.

'You, Malphus, go to this side, and, Mendis, come along with me,' Dimitri ordered and they moved on to search for Theodore. Jonathan and Zoran were already in the jungle for the search. Everyone was shouting 'Theodore!' and moving forward, when all of a sudden, Malphus shouted, 'Dimitri, Dimitri. Come here!'

Everyone ran towards Malphus. Dimitri was kneeling down and taking out something from the ground while Malphus was standing just near him.

Jonathan moved towards Dimitri and saw that Dimitri was touching a thick white liquid spread on a piece of rock.

'It is the blood of the giants of Gorgothon. Theodore must have fought well with them,' Dimitri said.

'Prepare for the invasion, we are going to the village Gorgothon,' Zoran thundered.

Everyone rushed towards the bonfire. Zoran, Malphus, and Dimitri took their weapons and instruments. Dimitri took two long swords and passed it over to Mendis and Jonathan. Mendis looked at the sharp sword that was shining bright like silver.

'I didn't want it this way. The giants, prepared, are much more dangerous. I was thinking of attacking them in the night and take the Buried Belt. But now they will have to pay for taking the son of Great Andrew Blake,' Dimitri said and jumped on to his horse. Now they were going much faster than usual.

They were now moving away from the river and Dimitri with Zoran was leading the pistol run. Soon after getting away from the river, the jungle was left behind. Now there was long and wide grassland in front of them. The grassland was not plain at all but somewhat providing an easy ride for all of them. The breeze was pleasant and cold. After moving for long in the grassland, Dimitri started slowing down. In front of them, it was looking like a dead end. Dimitri and Zoran were moving towards it.

It was not a dead end. It was almost a vertical slope leading to a plain field, which was the village of Gorgothon. There were a number of huts all around the village, which were quite big. Bonfire was on its verge at several places. Giants were sitting in groups at several places, some were fighting for a loaf of bread, piece of meat, some were carrying a lot of woods, and some were cutting it. It was all looking like a village of demons. At the center of the village, a giant was sitting on a wooden throne and was screaming at other giants continuously. He was having a long scar on his forehead and his right hand was tied with a plank. All of a sudden, Malphus saw Theodore lying beside the giant on the throne, wrapped in coconut rope, and was badly injured.

There was also a very strange thing in the village. There was a huge pond at the left-hand side of the village, while there was no source of it.

'This is the pond under which the Buried Belt is placed. Two of the huge pieces of rock are joined by the Buried Belt to stop the flow of water and to form this pond, which is used by the giants to grow Prytpus Plant, which they use to make the dead giants alive. That's why they are so much powerful and can never die. But only if the plant is fed to the giants before the first moon rises after their death,' Zoran said.

As Dimitri with the others were watching the village from above the cliff, five of the giants, running towards them, banged all of them from the back and they started rolling down with their horses towards the barren field. Fall of Dimitri and the others drew giant's attention. They were attacked by some giants on the cliff due to which they rolled down the ground, but somehow Zoran was able to escape from the ramming. They all fell down on the ground and Dimitri looked towards Zoran who was escaping from the place. Dimitri looked towards him and nodded his head.

The giant on the throne stood up in surprise. Now they were on their feet and surrounded by the giants who were screaming and howling loudly. One of the giants moved towards Malphus. Malphus rotated his mace from behind and rammed the giant coming towards him. He fell on ground and every other giant attacked them. Dimitri with his hammer was knocking the giants one by one, while Malphus was trying to protect Mendis and Jonathan who were not able to do much with their swords. The number of giants moving towards them was much more than the count of giants being knocked down. They were huge, outnumbered, and most importantly, were mad. It was looking like a never-ending flow of monsters towards them. All of a sudden, a giant picked up Jonathan into his hand, seeing which Mendis bravely entered the sword into the giant's ankle and he winced, throwing Jonathan aside.

'Move, move, you morons, pay respect to our visitors,' the giant with the scar sneered, making way for himself, pushing the giants aside.

'Let Theodore go!' Dimitri thundered, clinching his hammer.

'Oh, his name is Theodore, the son of Great Andrew Blake. He is brave, but not powerful,' the giant uttered.

'We will take back Theodore and the Buried Belt with us,' Dimitri said.

'Oh, another journey and an attempt to take the Buried Belt and other two powers. I can't understand why you musicians can't accept that the Blood Shredder can't be brought back. The Buried Belt is in our village from the past four years and no one can take it. Those mad three—'

'Don't disrespect The Three!' Malphus screamed and jumped towards the giant, but with just a flick of his hand, he banged Malphus on the ground.

'I want to fight with you, little Nimbler, and if you win, I will give you back Theodore and the Buried Belt. My revenge of this scar and broken hand by one of your types will end today,' the giant said and challenged.

'You have done the biggest mistake of your life,' Dimitri warned, clinching his hammer.

'Look at the little Nimbler, he is going to piss in his pant,' the giant chuckled and Dimitri pushed Jonathan and Mendis aside.

'Make some room for the grave of this little fairy tale,' the giant said and every other giant moved aside.

Dimitri ran towards the giant. As the giant tried to bang him with his hand, Dimitri dodged it and jumped onto his knee; the giant hit again, Dimitri dodged and climbed to his waist. The giant on the verge of his patience hit forcefully on Dimitri, but this time he also managed to dodge and jumped into the air. Dimitri rammed the giant onto this face with the hammer while swooping down and landed perfectly on the ground.

The giant howled with pain and grabbed Dimitri from the ground.

'You!' the giant growled, looking into Dimitri's eyes and threw him on the ground. Dimitri fell like a piece of rock on the ground and rolled down to some distance. As Dimitri was trying to control himself, the giant pushed him deep into the vertical cliff and started punching him deep into it like a punching bag. One, two, three, the other giants started counting the punches.

After six or seven punches, the giant stopped and Dimitri fell from the hole made by the punches like a dead body. His clothes were colored in blood. His whole body was covered in dirt and was bleeding from his mouth.

'Dimitri!' Jonathan and Mendis screamed but were helpless and were in the grab of those giants.

Dimitri tried to stand up but was looking powerless and fell again.

'Ha. This little Nimbler was going to defeat me. I think they have forgotten how their village was snatched from them by the monsters. Their women were raped, houses burnt, men killed, and they were not able to fight back. They were made slaves on their own land. If those musicians wouldn't have come for help, they would still have been slaves.' The giant laughed and kicked Dimitri.

Dimitri was hearing all the things and was boiling with anger. These words were acting as a catalyst in gaining his lost energy.

'Look at you, still helpless, living as a worker in Riffsland and still not able to protect themselves on their own. What a life. Even the prisoners at Market of Cheaters live a better life than you.'

Dimitri tired to stand up but his legs were still shivering due to the pain.

'Even I was a part of that invasion and raped some of your women.' The giant chuckled.

Dimitri's hammer was now shining bright red like a molded iron. Even the giants were surprised by the glow of that hammer. Jonathan and Mendis were just staring at the hammer and were left speechless.

Dimitri, with whole body burning in the pain of his lost family, villagers, and the disrespect by the giant, was moving slowly towards the big giant. The giant, who was boastful just a second ago, went mum.

'Oh, your hammer looks angry like you.' The giant chuckled with a fake smile to overcome his fear and ran towards him. Dimitri started rotating his hammer, and as the giant came closer, Dimitri with just a single shot knocked the giant down.

'Kill him, kill him,' the knocked giant ordered the other giants, holding his bleeding nose and they ran towards Dimitri.

Dimitri pushed back his hammer with full force and banged it on the ground due to which sound of creaking started coming. Every giant stopped at his place, and all of a sudden, the ground started breaking into pieces and the giants started falling into the deep cracks made by the breaking of the ground. It was looking like an earthquake.

Dimitri took the fainted Malphus on his shoulder and gave him to Mendis to carry him away from the barren field, which was getting engulfed, while Jonathan with Theodore, who was made free by Dimitri, started climbing all the way up. The ground was breaking from many points and the earth was shaking.

Dimitri ran towards the pond and jumped into it. The big pieces of rocks were falling in the pond too, and Dimitri was trying to dodge them. As Dimitri went to the bottom of the pond, he found that the Buried Belt was not there. There was no sign of the two pieces of rock joined by anything, but there was only a big single piece of rock stopping the flow of water. There was also no Prytpus Plant in the pond. Dimitri was in shock and swam all the way up. He looked around and there was no way to get away from the ground. Every piece of ground was going down under the cracks, and all of a sudden, the bottom rock in the pond broke and water started flowing with force, which started pushing Dimitri with it. He was holding a sharp edge of the rock, but suddenly he lost the grip, but an arrow with long rope at its back fired by Zoran stuck right in front of him and Dimitri grabbed the arrow. Holding the arrow, Dimitri swung all the way to the vertical cliff and started climbing on it. As they were climbing up, some of the giants grabbed Jonathan and Mendis from behind, but all of a sudden, two arrows right into their eyes threw them back into the deep cracks. It was fired by Zoran from the top of the cliff. He fired another arrow, behind which a rope was tied. Jonathan with the others grabbed the rope, and just when the whole place was going to engulf, they managed to climb all the way up.

Somehow the giant with the scar with other two giants also managed to get away from the barren field and ran away from Dimitri.

'We should catch them,' Malphus said, but Dimitri caught his leg.

'No. Zoran, do it,' Dimitri said to Zoran, and Zoran took out two arrows from his back and pointed it sharply towards the running giant and fired it. One hit the ankle of a giant and one pierced through the arm of another giant. One of them looked behind, howled, and continued his run.

'That was huge. Till now I had only heard of it, but this was the first time I saw it. The Nimbler's Destruction,' Zoran said.

'It's not a controllable thing. It just comes out,' Dimitri wheezed.

'Are you all right?' Zoran asked Theodore, cutting the tied rope from his hand.

'Why didn't you chase them? They will have to pay for kidnapping me. I fought them well, but they outnumbered me,' Theodore growled.

'Calm down, boy,' Dimitri warned.

'The Buried Belt is also gone within the cracks,' Jonathan said, looking at the disaster caused by Dimitri.

'It's not there,' Dimitri said.

'What do you mean by it's not there?' Zoran asked.

'They faked the pond in their village. It's not there. They have hid it somewhere else and now they are going for it. We will follow them and take the Buried Belt,' Dimitri said.

'And how we are going to follow them? They are out of our frame,' Mendis quizzed.

'These giants, when injured, spread a type of fragrance from their body to heal themselves and that fragrance is easy to smell,' Zoran said.

'That's why you injured him with your arrow,' Malphus said, holding his hand that was throbbing due to the bang.

'We have lost three horses and we are left with only three,' Malphus said, ruffling the horse.

'We will move in pairs,' Zoran said.

Zoran was with Mendis, Dimitri with Theodre, and Malphus with Jonathan on the three horses. Zoran was leading the troop by smelling the fragrance of giants like a dog. He was following the fragrance like a common man follows the direction marked by arrows. Dimitri was looking lost in his own thoughts. It must have been his revenge. It was very difficult for him to move from his village and adjust in Riffsland. The graves of his loved ones, family, villagers were still in his mind, and the giant with his words like venom scratched the wounds on Dimitri's heart.

'The pond is near, the fragrance is swelling,' Zoran said.

'I will kill the big one,' Theodore warned.

'Don't be foolish, even only three of them are very much dangerous,' Dimitri said.

'Hshhh, they are very near,' Zoran silenced everyone.

Now in front of them there was a big pond in the middle of the grassland. The sun was shining on it. But there was no sign of the giants. They looked here and there but no sign of the giants.

'The fragrance is at its peak,' Zoran said.

'But where are the giants?' Malphus asked.

'We must go near the pond,' Theodore said.

'No, it can be a trap. We will wait here,' Zoran said.

'Zoran is right. We will wait here,' Dimitri said and they stopped at the place where they were standing.

They kept waiting and waiting but no one came. Their patience was on its verge. Everyone was looking in all possible directions to get even a glimpse of those giants, but all they were able to see was the grassland and the pond.

'Nothing is going to happen. We can wait here for our whole life but no one will come,' Theodore said.

'I think we should take the first step,' Malphus suggested.

'Okay,' Dimitri said and they jumped off from their horses.

Zoran was leading. They were moving slowly towards the pond and looking everywhere for any sign of the giants. Zoran reached near the pond and said, 'Look', pointing towards the molted skin.

'What is this?' Malphus asked.

'It looks like a molted skin and the smell is coming from it. How could they do it in this season? They were able to molt in winter only,' Zoran quizzed.

'They knew that we will follow them for the fragrance and they molted here so that we will stop at this pond,' Dimitri said.

'It means that they have taken the Buried Belt,' Jonathan gasped.

'No, no. All the three powers are very much powerful and can't be controlled by anyone until the black moon arrives, which comes once in five years. On that night, all the three powers can be transferred for which every living creature outside the walls of Riffsland fights for. And those who gets it becomes its possessor till the next black moon. Only the String of Snakes can be moved, but only the island could be changed, not the possession till the black moon. But there is a curse that if a musician will win these powers on the night of black moon and bring it to his city, his whole city will be engulfed by disasters. That's why we were not able to get it on black moon,' Zoran said.

'So this means I am the one who can control these three powers without the black moon?' Jonathan said.

'Yes, because you were able to break the stone of Blood Shredder, we knew that you can control these powers.'

'But the Blood Shredder belongs to me', Theodore snapped, 'once we will bring all the three powers to Riffsland, I will bring back the Blood Shredder and my mom will wake up from her sleep.'

'Let's go, Jonathan. Me and Malphus will go with you in the pond and rest of you will look after us,' Zoran said, taking his boots off.

Jonathan, Malphus, and Zoran jumped into the pond. The pond was very muddy and visibility under it was very less. Zoran signaled Jonathan to go down with him, while Malphus was looking for the belt above. Zoran and Jonathan swam all the way down to the bottom of the pond. Zoran signaled Jonathan to look for the belt on the other side. The water was very muddy and the bottom was very slippery. There were similar green plants all over the base. Gripping on the rocks in the base, Jonathan started moving towards the wall when suddenly he felt someone was behind him. He turned around, but no one was there. He again started moving forward. Zoran was out of the frame now and Jonathan was feeling scared, deep under the muddy pond.

As Jonathan grabbed a rock to move forward, the rock slipped from its place and Jonathan saw something glittering on the side. He moved towards it and it was the Buried Belt. It was holding two huge rocks that were stopping the water to flow away. The Buried Belt was covered in mud but was still glittering. Jonathan, with curiosity, swum towards the belt, and as he touched it, someone pushed him back.

Jonathan turned around and it was the giant. His skin was looking new and soft. Jonathan pushed the giant away with his leg, but he grabbed it again and punched Jonathan, right on to his nose. Jonathan started bleeding and tried to move away from the giant, but the giant was looking much more comfortable underwater than Jonathan. He grabbed Jonathan's neck and clinched it. Jonathan was losing his breath and his vision started to blur, but from the muddy water, someone hit back at the giant. It was Zoran. He grabbed the giant's head that distracted him from Jonathan. The giant swung his head to push away Zoran, but his grab was tight.

Seeing the shake in the water, as Dimitri went near the pond, Malphus with another giant jumped off from the pond. The giant fell on the side of the pond while Malphus landed safely. The giant's skin was soft and was wet because of the molting. As he came out of the water, his skin started burning, and just in seconds, his whole body turned into ashes.

'They are still inside the pond with another giant!' Malphus screamed.

'Wait a second. There were three giants who escaped from Gorgothon. One you killed, one is under the water, so where is the third one?' Mendis said.

'There are only two molted skins,' Theodore said, looking at the molted skin.

'Move,' Dimitri squealed, pushing Mendis aside.

It was the third giant behind Mendis who tried to hit him with a big trunk of a tree.

'Malphus, jump into the pond and help them. We will take care of him,' Dimitri ordered and Malphus again jumped into the pond.

The third giant with trunk in hand ran towards Mendis and swung his trunk to hit Mendis. Mendis closed his eyes, the sound of trunk swinging in the air blew up in his near, the whisperer clinched Mendis's jacket, and it passed, but Mendis was still standing.

It was Theodore who cut the trunk with his axe. Mendis opened his eyes and the piece of trunk was lying on the ground at some distance. The giant howled and threw the remaining piece of trunk towards Theodore, which he chopped like a piece of paper.

Under the water, Zoran was fighting with the giant and was still holding his head, but all of a sudden, the giant got a broken piece of rock. Zoran looked at the piece of rock in the giant's hand, closed his eyes covering his face with his hand, and the giant rammed Zoran with it.

He then moved towards Jonathan who was fainting slowly. As the giant reached towards Jonathan, Malphus, out of the blue, entered his mace into the giant's hand and he winced. Malphus got the chance and took Jonathan on his shoulder and swum all the way up. As he put Jonathan on the side, he again got pulled inside the pond by the giant. Malphus tried to hit him with his mace, but the giant flicked it away. Now Malphus was bare-handed and in the grip of giant.

On the land, the giant now rushed towards Theodore, and Theodore took grip on the ground with his leg, positioning his axe to attack. The giant was speeding up and Theodore was still standing. Theodore was looking directly into the eyes of the giant, thirty, twenty, ten feet away, and as the giant reached near Theodore, Dimitri slammed his hammer onto his leg, and as he fell, he got returned by a heavy hit by Theodore from his axe. The giant jumped into the air and fell some distance away from them.

Under the water, the giant's neck was under the grip of Zoran's bow and Malphus was in the giant's grab. The tightening on the giant's neck by Zoran was being transferred to Malphus who was feeling like his rib was going to break. All of a sudden, the giant flicked his neck and Zoran fell in the corner of the pond. The giant howled and bubbles came out of his mouth. He then threw Malphus on Zoran who was just moving away from the corner. The giant then took a big piece of rock, and as he was going to throw it at them, the water started decreasing. The force was huge and everything started moving with it. It was Jonathan who removed the Buried Belt with him, and all the water was now moving into the hole due to the gap made because of the two big pieces of rock. Jonathan hung the Buried Belt, holding which both Zoran and Malphus swam all the way up. The giant made grip on one of the rocks, but the force of the water was huge. He looked glumly at Jonathan and others swimming all the way up with the Buried Belt. The water was passing by the hole with a huge force and the giant was losing his grip. He lost the first rock and then held another, but this time even the rock slipped out of the ground, and with the rock, he got engulfed in the hole.

On the ground, Theodore and Dimitri were still fighting with the giant when Dimitri ended the battle by his final shot, deep into the head of the giant, and he fell on the ground.

'Never underestimate a Nimbler,' Dimitri said, putting his feet on the giant's face.

The pond was now empty with little water left on the base. The similar-looking plants at the bottom started dying and the water passed by the hole.

'The Buried Belt,' Mendis shouted, seeing it in the hands of Jonathan.

'Yes, yes, we have got it,' Jonathan wheezed.

Dimitri looked towards the Buried Belt. It was the best belt Zoran had ever seen in his life. It was black in color with gold and silver colored art on it. And there was a magnificent art of a lion's and eagle's heads on both of its side.

Theodore moved slowly towards the Buried Belt and took it from the hands of Jonathan who was still lying on ground and trying to breathe all the air in the atmosphere.

'It's marvelous. I have never seen such a belt in my life,' Theodore mumbled.

'I knew that you are the one who will move these three powers. You did it, Jonathan. Now we will be able to bring back the Blood Shredder,' Zoran said, getting up from the ground.

'It's truly amazing,' Mendis said, coming closer to Theodore who was still looking at the beauty and power of the belt.

'How did he die?' Zoran asked, looking at the ashes of the giant.

'I think after molting, two giants whom we injured went into the pond because their new skin needs coldness. But when he was thrown away by Malphus, his skin burnt in the sun,' Dimitri said.

'Let me see,' Zoran asked for the Buried Belt and took it in his hand. He was also stunned by the power and beauty of that belt and he could feel a field of force around it.

'Keep it, Theodore. One gone, two to go,' Zoran said, handing over the Buried Belt to Theodore.

CHAPTER SEVENTEEN

THUNDERING MOUNTAIN

Dimitri was looking at the Red Paper on the horse, behind which Malphus was sitting. The long grassland was about to end, and in front of them was a series of mountains. But still the mountains were far from their reach. In between the grassland and the mountains, there was a long barren field. In between the series of mountains, there was a giant mountain that was looking green and covered in fog and dark cloud was hovering over it, while the other mountains were shining in the bright sunlight and were not as high as that one.

'That is our destiny,' Dimitri said, looking at the mountains.

'Which one? The mountains?' Theodore asked.

'The one in the middle, covered in clouds.'

'Is that the place where dragons live?' Mendis asked.

'Oh, the Thundering Mountain, this is the home of all the dragons,' Malphus said.

'I think that's why Zorich selected you for the journey. Your specialization has always been the subject of dragons,' Zoran said.

'Yeah, Malphus is a genius when it comes to dragons and he knows all the things about them,' Dimitri said.

'I have read about the Thundering Mountain in the books and the way Sir Jack Thomas, the master of dragons, has explained it, it looks exactly the same.' Malphus sighed.

'But why has it been named as Thundering Mountain?' Mendis interrupted Malphus's uncontrollable emotions.

'The black cloud on the mountain never leaves it. But these clouds never rain, they only thunder at night which is the reason of its name,' Malphus explained.

'Let's move on,' Zoran said and they moved towards the barren field.

'Finally the thing for which I was waiting for my whole life,' Malphus mumbled while moving away.

Malphus was continuously moving towards the Thundering Mountain and his eyes were showing a dream that he was not ready to share with anyone. Everyone was surprised by the Thundering Mountain, but Malphus's emotions were different. Jonathan always used to say to Mendis that Malphus is very confusing and looks like a freak, but Mendis didn't give this topic much importance because for him even Zoran was a freak.

'It is going to be one of the most difficult powers to conquer,' Zoran said.

'Why?' Mendis asked.

'You heard that after every five years, all the living creatures fight for these three powers. So that their type will be blessed with something very good, like in the case of giants, it was the Platypus Plants. But from the past twenty years, no one has been able to win over these dragons and the pick belongs to them from the past twenty years. Many powerful tribes, monsters, and giants have tried to fight with them on the night of black moon and win the pick, but no one has ever succeeded.'

Mendis swallowed and said, 'And we are going to get it.'

Going through the barren field, it was all dark again, and the Thundering Mountain with black clouds roaming on it was looking huge and blood-curdling. Dimitri without taking rest for the night decided to climb the mountain. The mountain was almost vertical, and there was no way to climb the mountain with the horses.

'We need to leave our horses here,' Zoran said.

'And what will happen to them?' Mendis asked.

'We will send a message on them and they will return to Riffsland,' Zoran said.

'Will they?' Jonathan asked suspiciously and Dimitri twitched his shoulder.

They got off from their horses, fed them for the last time, and Zoran took out a plectrum from his pocket and started writing something on the horse, which was not visible. It was like writing with a pen without ink. He wrote on every horse. Dimitri touched every horse and mumbled something. The whisperer on Mendis's shoulder was looking curiously at what was happening. Finally after writing on every horse and mumbling something by touching them, Malphus pushed them away, shouting, 'Go, Go. Thoron. Thoron.'

And the horses ran back towards the grassland. Now they were on their feet and the mountain was very high and looking impossible to climb. They were not having any rope or way to climb the mountain and were still ready to go on the top. As Jonathan moved towards the Thundering Mountain, which was in front of them, Dimitri stopped him, saying, 'This is not the mountain which we are going to climb.'

'But this is the Thundering Mountain where the Pick of Dragon is,' Jonathan cross-questioned.

'Yeah, but no one can climb on the Thundering Mountain. The dragons keep flying all over it, and once they see us, they will pick us up, move all the way up, and then drop us,' Malphus said.

'So?' Theodore asked.

'We will be going from the mountain near it,' Malphus said, pointing towards a mountain next to it.

'Is there any way which connects the two mountains because it looks like these two mountains are much apart from each other,' Mendis asked suspiciously.

'Yes, a bridge.'

'A bridge on the top of mountain near the Thundering Mountain.' Jonathan gaped.

The sun was about to vanish and they were in the middle of the mountain. This mountain was easy to climb because of the man-made path that was leading all the way up to the top. The suspicious bridge on the top, these paths that were making the tracking easy were a straight sign that someone before them had also climbed these mountains. Jonathan was thinking that the bridge, these paths may have been made by the one whom Malphus was talking about, master of dragons, Sir Thomas. Although Jonathan didn't know anything about Sir Thomas but the way Malphus took his name, it looked like Sir Thomas was a legend.

In between the paths, there were many signboards, covered with plants, algae, and only their shape could be predicted, which was rectangular. Malphus was leading the troop and Jonathan was just behind him when Malphus stopped at one of the signboards. He moved towards the board, took his small knife, and cleaned the plants to read the board. It was written, 'BASE-21.'

'What's base 21?' Jonathan asked.

'The base at the top of mountain is 21 red dragons away,' Malphus said.

'Red dragons?'

'Yes, they used to measure distance on the basis of red dragons. One dragon means 100 meters and this sign means that the base is still 21 red dragons away.'

'That's a strange way to measure distance.'

'The hole must be here, we can't move at night. It's too dangerous,' Malphus said, looking up for something into the rocks.

'What are you looking for?' Mendis shouted from behind, feeling tired after climbing half of the mountain, fighting with giants, and dealing with the Cheaters.

'He must be looking for the rest point which was supposed to be at BASE-21, clever boy.' Zoran chuckled.

'Yes, there it is!' Malphus exclaimed.

As Malphus cleared the grasses from the rock, the reason for Malphus's glee was visible. It was a small cave with enough space for all of them. Although it was looking very dark inside and possibilities of treacherous creatures inside it was stopping Jonathan to move towards it. But as said by Maphus, it was very dangerous to move in the night at Thundering Mountain, this cave was nonetheless a lifesaving point.

'Are we really going to step into it?' Mendis asked, looking at the dark cave when everyone gathered around it.

'Yes, they are safe, made by the troops of Sir Thomas,' Malphus said confidently.

'He must be a brave man because making a cave at such a height is not a cakewalk,' Mendis appraised Sir Thomas.

'The bridge is also made by him and his troops,' Dimitri said, moving towards the cave.

Jonathan and Mendis were just left gaping at what Dimitri just said. Climbing such a mountain, when no paths were there, was itself a big challenge and making a bridge that connects this mountain to Thundering Mountain was just unbelievable. Jonathan and Mendis were having many questions in their minds and this journey was revealing many hidden legends, creatures, and enemies for them. But putting all these questions aside, in front of them was the dark cave in which they were supposed to sleep at night.

'Why are you so much scared? I am going in, once I will signal, everyone will come then,' Zoran said, taking a small knife out.

Everyone was looking curiously at each step of Zoran. He slowly slid towards the cave, making grip on the base. He stood at the cave and peered inside. He then turned his head backwards towards them with an expression of disappointment and Mendis thought what Zoran imagined, he will look inside the cave and will get crystal-clear view of everything.

Zoran trudged slowly towards the down-slopping cave and entered into it. Everything came at a pause and everyone was looking towards the pitch-dark and eerie cave curiously with an expectation of signal from Zoran, but it was looking like he got lost into the darkness.

All of a sudden, a large flock of bats flew away from the cave that made everyone standing outside to either jump or move aside.

'There is a flambeau inside the cave,' Zoran said from inside the cave but still he was not visible.

Sound of something being lit came and the whole cave was now visible. Zoran was standing in the cave with the lit flambeau in his hand.

'Come inside, it's safe,' Zoran said confidently.

Everyone following Malphus trudged down the cave. It was not very deep as it was looking from outside. The space was enough for not more than ten men. Taking the lit flambeau, Zoran lit another one, which was hanging just opposite to it.

'This is the cave of BASE-21. What a piece of marvel at such a point of height. Sir Thomas said that one day someone will come and end the possession of these dragons. For those he made these paths, cave, bridge, so that he can give his maximum to the future possessor of Pick of Dragon from our kingdom and he had done it in the best way a man on earth could do,' Malphus drawled.

'Are we going to spend the whole night here?' Mendis asked, touching and pushing the walls for some more surprises.

'Yes, we are, because at night, the dragons wander around the whole mountain, and if they would get to know about us, I bet that we will not be able to move a single inch from here,' Zoran said, trying to make a comfortable base on the rocky ground.

'Do they sleep at daytime?' Jonathan asked.

'No, there are hundreds of species of these dragons and each has a different trait. Most of them sleep at night, but the Nightwalkers sleep at daytime and protects the mountain from traitors at night,' Malphus said.

'So they are the one from which we are hiding,' Mendis added.

'Yes, they are the most dangerous one. Every dragon is dangerous, but the Nightwalkers are considered in the top ten. They can see as clear at night as an eagle can see at daytime. And they can easily hide their gigantic body at night, which makes them much more dangerous. It is written in the books that after the Camouflaged dragons, they are the best at hiding. As like every other dragon, they also throw fire from their mouth, but at night that fire looks blue in color and vanishes anyone just in a fraction of a second.' Malphus was trying to summon up everything he has read throughout his life in just one night.

'It will be better if we lit only one flambeau because we need just a source of light without making our presence known to the Nightwalkers,' Dimitri said and put out one of the flambeau.

The cave was just near the top of the mountain or what according to Sir Thomas, just 21 red dragons apart. At such a height, the cold breeze was making it difficult to sleep and the mind-blowing story told by Malphus about the Nightwalkers was adding taste to the blood-curdling night. Jonathan was looking at the whisperer in Mendis's arms who always managed to sleep well. Whether it is a forest, top of mountain, he slept very calmly and happily. Jonathan always tried to do so, but he was not a whisperer. Jonathan came to know about this happy sleeping quality of whisperers from his own experience by being awakened for many nights on the journey.

Jonathan was very much surprised that instead of him everyone was sleeping. He was expecting at least one person to remain awake, seeing whom he could have got some hope. The sound of thundering from the near mountain was making the night more dreadful for Jonathan. He was thinking about Sivur that he would come and take him again to a safe place to sleep.

He again lay down and closed his eyes, but then he heard something passing by. He stood up and looked at the opening of the cave. No one was there. He then turned around and again closed his eyes and this time a big shadow passed on the wall in front of him.

He took his sword given by Dimitri, which he didn't know how to use, and slowly stepped towards the opening of the cave. It was a foolish act, but he didn't wake anyone and found it better to look at the thing by himself and it was like he got used to it. Trying to look in every direction, he slowly moved out of the cave, but still nothing was there. The cold breezes were more chilling outside, and at such a height, the night was looking very frightening. The lightning from the near mountain was sounding very blood-curdling. As after checking in every direction when Jonathan was on his way back to the cave, someone rammed him from the left and they both rolled into the bushes. Jonathan was on the ground and the one who rammed him was just sitting above him, trying to smother. As Jonathan pushed him away, he saw that it was Malphus. In the cave, he was so much worried about his sleepless night and the sound of lightning that he forgot that Malphus was not there in the cave.

'What are you doing here?' Jonathan whispered.

'Shut your mouth,' Malphus hissed and pointed towards the gigantic dragon hovering over the mountain.

It was the Nightwalker. Seeing the dragon, Jonathan realized that the story by Malphus about this dragon was just a glimpse to what he looked like in the glittering moonlight.

Rocky body, shining white eyes, and flying in the dark night so swiftly that even the wind crossing through his wings couldn't be heard. It took some seconds for his shadow to pass over Jonathan and Malphus. With Malphus sitting on his back, lying on the ground, Jonathan was gaping at the mesmerizing view of Nightwalker in the bright moonlight.

'He is really big and amazing,' Jonathan whispered.

'Crawl slowly towards the cave and don't make any sound,' Malphus hissed.

Moving off from Jonathan's chest, Malphus started crawling towards the cave and signaled Jonathan to do the same. Looking at the sky, Malphus was slowly moving towards the cave and Jonathan was doing the same, when grudgingly, Jonathan stepped onto a slippery rock, and toppling badly, he rolled down, taking Malphus with him, down the ground, just near to the cave into the bushes. The sound due to the slip was enough to be heard, and as expected, hiding into the bushes they saw a Nightwalker coming back towards the cave. He landed slowly and started searching for them. He was now looking much bigger and dangerous. Jonathan and Malphus shrunk against the wall and were frightened to death. Malphus pushed Jonathan towards the wall. But this was not it. Following the first Nightwalker, two more landed there.

Each Nightwalker was searching in different directions and one of them was coming just towards the bushes where Jonathan and Malphus were shivering and petrified. The Nightwalker was coming closer and closer. They smothered themselves to make their presence unknown. The Nightwalker came closer, looked into the bushes, and moved back. He slowly moved towards the cliff and dived into the air, following whom, the other two Nightwalkers also flew away.

Jonathan fell on the ground, breathing the air of relief.

'That was really close.' Jonathan sighed.

'From next time, stop being so foolish,' Malphus said hotly, moving towards the cave.

'I knew that you were mysterious, but what was that?' Jonathan asked.

'It's none of your business,' Malphus miffed.

'All those weird things you do, the way you speak. I know that there is something wrong with you and I will tell it to the others,' Jonathan said and started moving towards the cave when Mendis pushed him on the walls and snapped, putting a knife on his neck.

'Do you think that the others will believe this story of yours? It will not only end the journey, but will also end you and your friend's life,' Malphus said, pushing Jonathan away.

'One day I will uncover your mask of mystery and everybody will see your real face of personal motives.'

Next morning was not good for Jonathan. His ankle was paining due to the last night's toppling. He woke up and saw everybody was awake. As he tried to get up, he howled with pain.

'What happened?' Dimitri asked.

'Are you all right?' Mendis said, coming closer to Jonathan and the whisperer jumped off from Mendis's shoulder.

'My ankle is paining badly,' Jonathan whined.

'Crying like a girl because of pain, thank God you are not an Riffslandn or you would have been a big black spot on Riffsland,' Theodore miffed, taking his jacket that he lay down to sleep upon.

'Sometimes the mistake and pain is realized later after its happening,' Malphus sneered, scowling at Jonathan.

'Here, take these,' Zoran said, entering into the cave and poring over some white-colored fruits kept in his pouch of jacket.

'What are these?' Mendis asked, taking one of the fruits.

'Oh, you found the Bloom Berry. They are found on high mountains and are full of nutrients and proteins which will be enough till the top,' Malphus said.

'It's tasty,' Mendis said, taking a bite of Bloom Berry.

'Finally we got something tasty to eat,' Jonathan said, holding his ankle and trying to move towards Mendis.

After eating the Bloom Berry, they were ready to cover the remaining distance to reach the top of the mountain. The whisperer jumped onto Mendis's shoulder, which was his new place to be, although he wasn't able to bear the stench coming off from Mendis's clothes that went through all the nasty things and was covered with dust, mud, and everything, which were enough to make the clothes stink.

Jonathan's ankle pain was decreasing and was now able to move towards the top without any support. Although Theodore was not happy about Zoran's idea of helping Jonathan in climbing the mountain, it was an order and he was supposed to follow. Theodore was still thinking about Jonathan's ankle pain and how he got it. He also looked at Malphus's expression when he heard about it.

The sun was shining bright, but the Thundering Mountain was still covered in dark clouds hovering over it. The brightening sunshine at one mountain and dark clouds at another was an awe-inspiring view.

Mendis was just behind Zoran, who was leading the early morning climbing. Jonathan was trying to get near to Mendis, who was after Dimitri and Theodore, moving in front of them. Moving away from the path, Jonathan reached near Mendis.

'Oh, why are you in so much hurry?' Dimitri said when Jonathan jostled to reach near Mendis.

'Sorry, Dimitri,' Jonathan muttered.

'Oh, how's your ankle pain?' Mendis asked when he saw Jonathan was just behind him.

'I need to tell you about something,' Jonathan whispered, looking here and there.

'About what?'

'Yesterday, when I was sleeping, I stepped outside the cave and saw Malphus was also out there. Then the Nightwalkers came there.'

'What? Nightwalkers,' Mendis spluttered.

'Shut your mouth. Three Nightwalkers came there and we hid into the bushes. Then they flew away.'

'Why didn't you tell it to anybody?'

'This is the important thing. When I said Malphus to tell it to everybody, he warned me not to.'

'Why?'

'I don't know.'

'So what do you think? We should tell it to others.'

'I think we will keep it as a secret between you and me and we will look upon this by ourselves,' Jonathan said, looking at the whisperer.

'Oh, don't take tension about him. He is on our side,' Mendis said and the whisperer nodded his head.

Zoran was about to grab the ground on the top of the mountain and everyone was waiting behind him as the path from where they were standing to Zoran was very dangerous to climb. At the start, Mendis requested that he will check the path for safety, but putting him aside, Zoran chose to go. Jonathan always used to think that how can a man like Zoran who was ready to go for any unknown place which was full of danger could be frightened of butterflies. Jonathan knew that Zoran always tried to be tough, but he was not so.

For that small way of nearly three hundred meters, it took a legend like Zoran thirty minutes to climb, and clambering slowly, now finally he was just a push away from the top of the mountain. He somehow scrambled to the top and lay on the ground fainting.

'What's up there?' Malphus shouted from the bottom loudly with excitement.

Zoran pulled himself up, and as he saw what was on the top of the mountain, he went speechless.

'What's there, Zoran?' Dimitri asked.

'You should come and see.' Zoran sighed.

In excitement, pushing Mendis aside, who was just going to climb, Malphus rushed to the way.

Malphus was struggling to climb to the top when Zoran pulled him up and that was it. There was a big plane land on the top of the mountain, and in the middle of it, there was statue of man with a small dragon on his shoulder. He was having long beard and his boots were pointed. His one hand was pointing towards the east side and another one was holding a book. Around forty to fifty feet from the statue, the area was barren, covered with dead leaves, instead of which it was all dense forest. There were blue-colored trees around that statue and it looked like someone used to use this place as a camp. The barren field was surrounded by trees with blue leaves, which were very strange as throughout the mountain, there wasn't any blue tree and these blue trees were weird and a strange smell was coming from them. Those trees were planted very orderly in a circle, which was of course done by someone.

Malphus went speechless as he saw the statue and was just staring at it. Zoran for a second looked at Malphus and then the statue, both were still.

'Sir Thomas,' Malphus sighed.

'Yes, he is the one, and since no one has ever returned home from the Thundering Mountain, no one knew about the statue,' Zoran said.

'He looks marvelous. The father of dragons, who knew everything about dragons. Without him, no one could have ever come to know about the dragons. He was the first to climb this mountain, and in his book, which he wrote while being on this mountain for more than a month, he also mentioned about a bridge which was being constructed, and since he was left with only few men, he decided to safely send this book to Riffsland so that others could also know about dragons,' Malphus said.

'Yes, but no one knows whether the bridge is completed or not.'

Following Malphus and Zoran, others also reached the barren field on the top and everyone was amazed with the view.

'What are these trees?' Theodore asked, touching one of the blue trees.

'I have never seen such type of trees in my life and the smell coming out of it is very strange and weird,' Dimitri said.

'Yes, I've never studied about them in the books. If Sir Thomas would have planted it, he must have mentioned it in his book. But only the bridge is mentioned,' Malphus said.

'But don't forget that he sent the book by one of his disciples before he died and he was left with only two people including your dad,' Zoran said to Malphus.

'His dad? Your dad came with Sir Thomas to these mountains?' Mendis babbled.

'Yes, he was a dragon maniac just like me. He joined the journey to these mountains with Sir Thomas and other thirty people. But only the one with the book returned and rest went missing, including my dad.' Malphus sobbed.

'I am very sorry,' Mendis apologized.

'We should move to check whether the bridge is a myth or reality,' Dimitri said.

'It must be in the direction in which the statue of Sir Thomas is pointing,' Theodore said, staring at the statue.

'The kid is right,' Zoran said.

They all moved towards the direction in which the statue was pointing, which was towards the eastern side of the mountains. In the eastern side, the Thundering Mountain was located. Apart from the barren field around the statue, the jungle on the top was much dense. Dimitri was making way in the jungle by chopping plants with his sharpened knife and was leading the way to the east. By passing through the jungles, at last when Dimitri cut the last big leaf, which was obstructing their path, it was there, the bridge connecting the Thundering Mountain to the one on which they were. Only half of the bridge was visible and the other half was lost in clouds. The bridge was very old and almost broken from everywhere, but still it looked like it could be crossed. Even the wind was making the bridge to creak. The bridge was rickety, but there was no other way. They didn't even know whether the other half of the bridge, lost in clouds, is tied with a rope or was in a worst condition.

'Can someone pass this bridge?' Jonathan said with bated breath.

And suddenly a plank of wood from the bottom of the bridge fell down.

Zoran opened his mouth, swallowed, and then said, 'We don't have any other option, but not now. These dragons are not like any other creatures we've faced so far. We will stay here for some days, search which dragons are there, make a plan, wait for the right time, and then attack.'

'It means we will set our camp here?' Mendis asked, and his whisperer jumped off from his shoulder to see the bridge.

'Yes, we will have to,' Dimitri said and everyone started moving back instead of Malphus.

He was still looking at the bridge and the Thundering Mountain. He was looking at the Thundering Mountain in such a way that he was trying to find something. Jonathan and Mendis were glaring at him while returning. Dimitri called two or three times, but Malphus didn't hear and finally he went near him.

'What is wrong with you, kid? Do you want the dragons to spot us? It will be much better if we keep hiding in the jungle until we come up with a proper plan,' Dimitri said hotly.

They all returned to the place where the statue of Sir Thomas was. The Thundering Mountain was not only the one on which dragons used to live. There were other species that were still undiscovered. There were more than ten species of them, but they kept on migrating from one mountain to another. There were eight to ten species that lived on each mountain and they kept on changing according to the season or sometimes randomly.

'How are we going to live on this mountain? If the dragons will spot us, they won't take a second to kill us,' Theodore said.

'First, we need to look upon which species are there because without knowing about them, we will not be able to judge their weakness, and for the question of living on this mountain, Sir Thomas did it for almost one month, so we can at least try it for three or four days,' Dimitri said.

'We have already seen Nightwalkers, and according to the season, the Camouflage dragons, Omnipotents, the one who carry the Pick of Dragon who are the weakest of all, and Bolt dragons would also be there,' Malphus said.

'You have seen a Nightwalker?' Theodore squealed.

'Actually when we were sleeping, I saw some of them from BASE-21's cave, flying on this mountain.'

'Oh, thank God you didn't step outside.' Theodore sighed.

'Look how he is lying; I think he is the one who forced them to come onto the ground. He is having something in his mind which is not looking good,' Jonathan whispered to Mendis.

'So we can spot the Camouflage dragon with some pest which I can easily make, Nightwalkers are a problem at night; for Ominpotents, we can't do anything instead of hiding in steeper areas; and for the Bolt ones, only God can save us,' Dimitri said.

'So we are all helpless,' Mendis said.

'But we still need to identify others, and the only way to do this is by going on to the Thundering Mountain through that creaked bridge,' Zoran said and looked towards the direction in which the bridge was.

Theodore looked in that direction, swallowed, and said, 'So whatever we do, we first need to pass that bridge.'

'Yes! But it's dawn now. We will cross that bridge in the morning. The cloud is much denser at that time,' Dimitri said.

'But the clouds are just an inch of advantage. It will wholly depend on our luck and courage,' Theodore added.

'And where are we going to stay for the night?' Malphus asked.

'And what if Nightwalkers come?' Jonathan said and gawked at Malphus who was looking at the statue.

'We will be sleeping in the circle of these blue trees and near to Sir Thomas. I hope his blessings save us from those dreadful dragons, and don't forget to cover yourself with these dead leaves. That will leave us with minimum chances of getting spotted,' Dimitri said.

'These Nightwalkers don't have very strong nose, but they can spot even the slightest of movements. So sleep like a dead body,' Malphus suggested.

As usual, in the blistering moonlight, Jonathan was still awake and waiting for Malphus's next move, and since Mendis was also a part of Jonathan's secret plan of identifying Malphus's night movements now, he was also awake. But there was no any movement by Malphus. He was sleeping in the opposite direction, but both Jonathan and Mendis were unaware that his eyes were wide open and shining. Mendis's whisperer was sleeping. Although he was also a part of this plan, but looking at his innocent sleeping face, Mendis was not able to wake him up. Everyone else was sleeping instead of these three.

'I think he is not going to do anything tonight,' Mendis whispered.

'Shut your mouth,' Jonathan said quietly.

'Can't you see that he is sleeping? We are wasting our time.'

'This is our only chance, and if you can't, you can go and sleep.'

'Look, I love sleeping but . . .,' Mendis said, paused for a moment, and then said again, 'He is gone.'

In between the useless conversation, they didn't notice that Malphus was gone and was not in the inner circle of the blue trees.

'I said to shut your mouth. Now let's go,' Jonathan snapped and they moved towards the jungle.

'Dimitri said to stay close to the statue,' Mendis said with bated breath.

'Look there he is hiding there, behind the tree,' Jonathan said hotly.

'But why is he hiding?' Mendis asked, taking cover of a tree.

'I don't know, but it must be related with the dragons.'

'I think it is related with his father.'

'A wild and useless guess,' Jonathan miffed.

Malphus was hiding behind a tree in a way like he was waiting for someone. He was standing still, and as he looked up, suddenly Jonathan's guess hit bull's-eye. A Nightwalker landed on the ground just near to Malphus. Malphus was still hiding behind the tree and looking at the Nightwalker who was touching something on the ground.

'Is that a real dragon?' Mendis sighed.

'Calm yourself, Mendis.'

'This is really big and beautiful, I mean dreadful, I mean strange. Ya, he is strange,' Mendis mumbled.

'Look he is crawling towards the Nightwalker,' Jonathan said.

'Hey, there is another one, but he is small.' Mendis pointed towards another dragon that landed close to the Nightwalker.

Because of the disturbance by the small dragon, Malphus stepped back towards the tree. It looked like the small dragon was not liked by the Nightwalker. As the small dragon came closer to him, the Nightwalker opened his mouth wide, signaling not to step forward. The small dragon shrunk himself as much as he could, but the Nightwalker was stepping towards him with aggressiveness. He was roaring at him continuously and finally the small dragon flew away from there. Following him after looking back, the Nightwalker also flew away.

Malphus was very much disappointed and was returning back to the statue, when all of a sudden, someone stepped in front of him from the trees. It was Jonathan and Mendis.

'So meeting with the Nightwalkers,' Jonathan said hotly.

'It's none of your business,' Malphus said coldly.

'You have to answer, otherwise we will tell it to the others,' Jonathan warned.

'Are you trying to threaten me? Do you think that Dimitri, Sir Zoran, and Theodore will believe on a hoax of yours and will have doubt on me?' Malphus said, pushed them away, and started moving.

'But we will find it out,' Mendis shouted.

'Why can't we tell it to the others?' Mendis asked while returning to the statue.

'Because we have no any proof. I thought tonight we will see what he does, but the small dragon spoiled everything and . . .' Jonathan paused, swallowed, and then said, 'Oh no.'

Dimitri was standing with Malphus while everyone else was sleeping. It was Malphus who woke Dimitri up and he was not looking happy. Jonathan and Mendis looked at each other and Dimitri said, 'So going against my instruction and wandering around at night.'

'But . . .,' Jonathan said, but Dimitri cut him off.

'This is the last time you are breaking my rules.'

'Yes,' Jonathan said, looking at Malphus who was still glancing at him.

'Now go back to sleep,' Dimitri said.

Next day started with a plan to cross the bridge as they didn't want to stay on the mountain for long. They didn't even know how they passed the first night without any dragons, but they also knew that luck would not always stay with them.

'So two of us will be holding the rope on this mountain, and the remaining three will be tying that rope around them and would cross the bridge. The last one would be on the tree and looking for the dragons, and as the cloud is very dense, so the one at the tree would signal as soon as possible,' Zoran said.

'Till now we only know about the four dragons on the mountain which are Nightwalkers, Camouflage, Omnipotents, and Bolt. Any other dragon will surely be a matter of surprise and only sudden decisions will save our life. So let's move on. May Sir Thomas's blessings be with us,' Dimitri said, kissing his locket.

Dimitri, Zoran, and Malphus were crossing the bridge, Jonathan and Theodore were holding the rope, and Mendis was on the trees. The whisperer was also holding the rope, although it didn't matter, but he didn't want to just sit on Mendis's shoulder.

The cloud was very dense at the bridge, and just after a minute, Dimitri, Zoran, and Malphus were lost in it. Theodore and Jonathan were holding the rope and were asked to pull the rope as fast as they could when they will hear anything from the Thundering Mountain. Mendis, trying to hide in the tree, was looking for dragons.

Dimitri was trying to look through the dense cloud as he was at the front. He was moving slowly as the bridge was rickety. Their every step on the bridge was making it creak. Both Zoran and Malphus were following the footsteps of Dimitri because not every part of the plank was that strong and falling from such a height would surely result in their demise.

Stepping slowly, now the Thundering Mountain started getting visible for Dimitri. It was full of greenery, and the way in which sunshine was falling from the steeper gaps between the cloud and trees, it was looking nothing less than heaven. But one thing was very much suspicious that still not even a single dragon was visible.

'It looks . . . it looks amazing,' Malphus mumbled.

'Just like heaven.' Zoran sighed.

'But no dragons,' Dimitri said suspiciously, and he stepped slowly on to the mountain, taking a deep breath of relief by crossing the bridge. Everyone opened his rope and tied it to a tree. They twitched the rope twice, signaling Jonathan and Theodore on the other side that they have reached.

Dimitri took out his hammer, Zoran took out his synth that turned into a bow and arrow, and Malphus took his violin that turned into a mace.

'Your art of creeping is amazing, even I am not able to understand where you are.' Dimitri chuckled, and as he looked backwards, Zoran and Malphus were not there and suddenly someone shouted from above.

'No!'

It was Zoran who was in grab of a dragon, Crippler, who was soaring high in the air.

Crippler was a very skinny and a white dragon with red eyes.

'Oh no, a Crippler,' Dimitri said and started running towards the flying dragon, but still Malphus was missing.

Zoran was trying to reach to his arrow, which due to the sudden grab by the Crippler, his arrow slipped away and now was hanging from his legs. But the Crippler, as the name suggested, liked to break legs and hands and was not in any mood of loosening the grip on him. Zoran was trying hard, but the grip was very strong. The dragon was taking very sharp turns across the tress in the jungle and was flying very fast, which Dimitri was trying to match and aim with his hammer.

All of a sudden, Zoran saw a tree that was enough in height for whatever plan he was thinking of. He shouted to Dimitri, 'The tree!'

And it was enough for Dimitri to understand. He jumped onto a rock and, aiming perfectly, threw his hammer, which passed tearing the tree like a paper. As the dragon saw the tree falling in his direction, he took a sharp 90-degree turn, which made him bent to the left. This sharp turn made Zoran to reach his arrow, which he jabbed as deep as he could into the dragon's body.

Screeching loudly, the Crippler loosened his grip on Zoran and he started falling with an abnormal speed. The speed was abnormal, Zoran was lurching, the ground was very near to him, when suddenly he took out his arrow and tangled it with one of the trees. Now Zoran was hanging in the air with his arrow tangled in a very high tree, but still it was a safe position than the dragon's grab.

'Where is Malphus?' Dimitri shouted.

'The Bolt!' Zoran shouted.

'Oh no,' Dimitri faltered.

And suddenly a very huge blow of air passed like a fired pistol.

'The Bolt,' Zoran whispered.

On the other mountain, Mendis was sitting on the tree and was still looking for the dragons when suddenly something very big passed by him, which almost blew him away from the tree. He was now dangling on the branch of tree.

'What was that?' Mendis mumbled.

And at last the Bolt was now visible who was soaring very high with Malphus in his grab who was looking almost fainted. The Bolt was having a very pointed nose with wings like jet plane and his whole body was black. He was not that big, which helped in his speed. For a second, Mendis went speechless, but believing in what he just saw, he shouted, 'The dragons, the dragons!'

As Jonathan and Theodore heard of Mendis, they pushed the rope, but it was still tied to the trees.

'They are still in the jungle,' Theodore said with bated breath.

Shouting of Mendis was enough to be heard by Dimitri, Zoran, and the other dragons, and as Zoran got on the ground, a bunch of Ticklevish, who were small in size in comparison to other dragons but still bigger than Dimitri and Zoran, flew towards them.

'Ticklevish. They will love to chew us away,' Zoran said frighteningly.

'Run towards the rope!' Dimitri shouted and they started running towards the bridge where the ropes were tied.

On the other mountain, where Jonathan and Theodore were still waiting for Dimitri, Zoran, and Malphus, Mendis somehow clambered on the top of the tree, but this time, luck was angry with him. As he reached on top of the tree and turned backwards, he saw the same Bolt coming towards him with Malphus in his grab. The pointed nails of the Bolt hung him like a hook and took him with Malphus up in the air. Mendis started shouting and was trying to wake up Malphus. The mace was still there, hanging from Malphus's hand. Mendis started pushing it.

Seeing Mendis up in the air with Malphus, Theodore left the rope in Jonathan's hand and ran towards the Bolt. Jonathan shouted to stop him, but he was not in any mood of holding the rope.

Speed of Bolt was lightning, and Mendis also started losing his conciseness. But one thing that Theodore noticed was that the Bolt was flying in the same path and every time he was crossing a cliff. Without wasting a single second, Theodore climbed onto the cliff, which was not much high, and positioned his axe into an attacking position. Looking at the Bolt, he was waiting. Looking into the Bolt's eyes, coming closer, closer, all ready to attack, and as the Bolt came in Theodor's range, he aimed perfectly and rammed him on the ground. Malphus and Mendis rolled down on the ground in different directions, while Theodore landed perfectly. The Bolt, screeching loudly, tried to fly, but his wings were injured. But Theodore didn't know that Bolt dragons were very good at running. Theodore hid behind a tree that fell when the Bolt banged it with its head.

Meanwhile Mendis and Malphus also got up on their feet and were now surrounding the Bolt.

On the Thundering Mountain, Dimitri and Zoran took the rope out of the tree, tied it around themselves, and as the Ticklers were just about to chew them apart, they ran on the bridge, which as expected, fell apart, and swinging towards the other mountain, both of them got rammed to it.

Jonathan started pulling them as fast as he can. He was struggling with two ropes, but somehow he managed to pull them on the top. As Dimitri and Zoran got on the top, they shouted, 'Run towards the jungle!'

And a huge wave of Ticklers, and this time with five Omnipotents above them, came from the clouds. Jonathan, Dimitri, and Zoran started running towards the jungle.

The Bolt also looked into the direction of the Thundering Mountain and then screeched loudly.

'I think we should run!' Malphus shouted to Theodore and Mendis.

They all were now running for their lives in the middle of the jungle and were unknown that they were running towards the statue of Sir Thomas.

They were running with a huge number of dragons behind them, and they finally reached near the statue.

The sound of wings and trees being ripped off for making the way was swelling and all of them were standing near the statue.

'We are going to die,' Mendis faltered.

'I am not sure about death, but I will fight till my last breath, which I am good at and which is under my control,' Dimitri said hotly.

Everyone took out their weapons and positioned themselves to attack, and the sound was swelling to its peak, when all of a sudden as the flock of dragons came closer to the blue trees or what we can say the barren land, they flew right up in the air taking a sharp turn of 90 degrees and everyone standing near the statue was amazed with their numbers that was covering the sky. They thought that they might come back and attack, but they flew away and the sound of wings faded.

'Where the hell are they going?' Theodore said, moving away from the statue and looking up in the air.

'I don't know, but we have got some more time to live and attack again,' Zoran said.

'I think either they don't like this place or something is related with this statue,' Malphus said and looked back at the statue.

'The trees. Yes, the trees. Can't you smell it? It is surrounding the whole place, these blue trees. From its order of being planted in a circle, it looks like a human with good knowledge of farming has done it,' Dimitri said, touching the blue trees.

'Sir Thomas. He must have planted these trees to protect himself and his adventurers from the dragon, but nothing about these blue trees is mentioned in his book,' Malphus said, staring at the blue trees.

'He sent his book very early since he feared getting killed by dragons, and no one would have been left to send the great information about these dragons. So when he was left with only two men, he sent his half-written book through one of them so the whole Riffsland could learn about dragons,' Dimitri said.

'It means that he must have planted these trees after sending his books. But if he was able to plant these trees, how he and others got killed?' Malphus asked suspiciously.

'He might have gone away from the boundary line of blue trees,' Mendis guessed.

'Yes, he might have, but he was a genius and he wouldn't have done such a thing,' Malphus said hotly.

'The number of dragons is much more than our expectation, and after an add up of Crippler and Ticklevish, now it has become much more difficult to get the Pick of Dragon,' Dimitri said.

'We were not even able to get near the Pick of Dragon or see it. How can we get such a thing?' Theodore miffed.

'Behave, Theodore. You are crossing your limits. When we started our journey, we had nothing, but now we have the Buried Belt with us. The time you lose hope, you kill yourself partially,' Zoran thundered.

'We will think about it, but from now, try to be as near to the blue trees as you can,' Dimitri said.

Till the time of dawn, everyone was tired with the attack, collecting woods for making food and other things. Everyone just wanted to sleep, but still moon was a little away. Some of them were lying on the ground and looking at the sky or just sitting around.

Maphus was sitting, taking the support of the statue on his back, when all of a sudden his eyes stuck at the left hand of the statue. There were six fingers in the left hand, but as much Malphus knew, Sir Thoms had six fingers in his right hand.

'Hey look, Mendis. Look, Sir Thomas had six fingers in his right hand, but the statue maker has mistakenly made six fingers in his left hand,' Malphus said to Mendis, who was passing by him, with hands full of woods.

'Instead of noticing the mistakes in the statue, if you will help us in collecting woods, it would be much more helpful,' Mendis miffed.

But Malphus ignored what Mendis said, touched the sixth finger in his left hand. He felt like the finger was rotatable. He rotated the finger made of plaster and it started coming out as a nut. And just after some seconds of rotation, it came fully out. Malphus was surprised and he touched the other fingers in his left hand of the statue, but none of them was rotatable. For a second, he thought to tell it to the others, but then words of Mendis came in his mind. He then looked at the right hand that was pointing towards the bridge. He saw that there was a space vacant near the thumb, and when he compared the size of the small hole and the plaster finger in his hand, it looked that both were the same. He took the finger and climbed on the statue. He then slowly fit the finger into the hole and it got fit like a glove. As he rotated the finger inwards, it got fixed properly.

'Hey, you will break the statue. What are you doing up there?' Theodore shouted.

'Nothing, nothing. Just checking the statue,' Malphus clarified and jumped off from the statue.

The night was haunting and numb. The thundering of clouds, blue trees, and the experience with dragons were making things worse. Malphus went away from the shades of blue trees and was waiting for Nightwalkers in the dark. But Jonathan and Mendis were also not frightened of Dimitri or Zoran because they wanted to know the truth by themselves.

As expected, just in some minutes, two giant Nightwalkers came on the ground and started checking something, which according to Mendis was put upon by Malphus. But this night turned out to be different, and Malphus, screaming loudly, taking his mace in hand, started running towards the Nightwalkers. It was looking like he just wanted to kill them, but there must have been something else than just the urge to kill them that faded the reality from Malphus's mind that no can kill such a giant dragon.

Seeing Malphus running with a mace, one of the Nightwalkers flew towards him, and with just a knock from his head, he banged Malphus to the trunk of the tree. Another Nightwalker also flew towards him. Malphus, holding his back, which was almost broken, tried to get near to his mace, but it was far apart.

'We should save him!' Mendis shouted and turned towards Jonathan, but he was not there.

Jonathan was running towards Malphus with the sword in his hand. Mendis also took his sword and ran towards Malphus.

When the Nightwalkers were just near to Malphus, the small dragon, which they saw the previous night, came flying from the air and hit one of the Nightwalkers, which was enough to distract him. Seeing the small dragon, both the Nightwalkers, leaving Malphus, flew towards him.

'Are you all right?' Jonathan asked, holding Malphus.

'The small dragon saved my life,' Malphus panted.

'They were just fighting. No one saved your life and what were you trying to do, kill a Nightwalker. Have you gone mad? Everybody says you are a master of dragons, but according to me, even a kid would be smart enough not to do what you did,' Mendis thundered.

'He killed my father and I wanted the revenge back,' Malphus growled.

'A Nightwalker killed your father?' Mendis asked surprisingly.

'Yes, everybody says that.'

'But no one knows the fact,' Jonathan added.

'Even in Sir Thomas's book, it has been mentioned that most of the people were killed by Nightwalker and I wanted revenge,' Malphus said furiously.

233

'But you can't kill a Nightwalker alone,' Mendis said softly, realizing that his guess at Malphus was wrong.

'You will never understand how it feels to see those dragons that killed my father. He was the one who loved them like anything, was passionate about them. He left my mother and me when I was just 8 to get with Sir Thomas and find the Thundering Mountain.' Malphus sighed.

'At least you could have told this before. Now get up, we need to go,' Jonathan said and picked up Malphus who was not able to stand properly.

'And thank you for coming to save me,' Malphus said as Jonathan picked him up.

'We were spying on you,' Mendis said coldly.

'Mendis,' Jonathan said hotly.

'But I am sure that small dragon came to save me. I saw him earlier also. He was being tortured by these ugly Nightwalkers and they forced him to fly away. It looks like they don't like the small one,' Malphus said on his way to the blue trees.

'You have gone mad. Why would a dragon save you? They all are from one family and they don't like humans. We have seen the results of getting near to them in the morning. I don't know what Dimitri is having in his mind and how will we get the Pick of Dragon,' Jonathan said.

The morning started with lot of shouting and it was by Mendis. He was shouting like a maniac for no reason. Everyone wanted to sleep a little more, but because Mendis was trying to wake everyone, some of them lost their temper.

'What on earth has forced you to wake us up?' Zoran growled.

'See, see. The sun is falling directly on the sixth finger,' Mendis babbled.

'Shut your mouth or I will throw you down,' Theodore miffed.

'It's falling on the stone and getting steeper,' Mendis spluttered.

'It's sunrise, so the sunrays would fall on stone. And you don't have a sixth finger, what's new about that?' Jonathan asked.

'No, no. Not my thumb. On the statue, on the statue.'

Jonathan finally woke, and when he saw the statue, he came to know about Mendis's excitement. The sunray was falling on the sixth finger of Sir Thomas's statue and was being sharply reflected back at a stone which was half under the ground and was very grubby. The stone was almost circular in shape.

Everyone woke up and was amazed by the reflection that was falling on the stone. It looked like it was not accidental. The statue was made with such intention, but one thing none of them were able to understand that this was not the first morning for them, then why it was reflecting the sunlight today.

'What the hell is this?' Dimitri whispered.

'Malphus, you were talking something about the sixth finger yesterday. Are you behind this?' Mendis asked.

'I just corrected the numbering of fingers. Sir Thomas had six fingers in his right hand, but in the statue, it was in his left hand. So I just made the correction,' Malphus said, staring at the reflection.

'It was not a mistake. It must have been made with some purpose. Which now we need to find,' Zoran said.

'Looks like this is not only the single piece of stone from which sunrays were made to pass. See there are gaps in series in front of the stone from which the sunrays is passing by,' Theodore said, getting closer to the circular stone.

'Look at the stone. It is not naturally circular. It has been carved into this form. Look at the cuttings on it,' Dimitri said, touching the circular stone.

'It is half below the ground, so there might be possibilities that the other stones in the series are under the ground,' Jonathan said.

'Let's dig,' Dimitri said and everyone took out his weapon for digging.

They started digging like machines and they were supposed to do it behind the blue trees because the blue trees were the only source of protection for them and they didn't want to rip them off.

Finally after an hour of digging, they found four same colored stones. All the stones were having different shapes, rectangular, triangle, pentagon, and the last one was irregular.

'In which series should we fix it?' Jonathan questioned, turning the pentagon stone in his hand.

'We should try it one by one,' Zoran suggested.

They firstly took the triangle one and put it in the series after the circular one, but the sunrays didn't pass by it. Then they took the pentagon one and this time the sunrays passed by, becoming much steeper. Trying one after another as they fixed the last stone on the series, the sunrays passed by it, which was looking thin like a thread. Passing by one stone after another, it was getting thinner and thinner.

After passing through the last stone, it was going beside the bushes in front of them. As Jonathan's sword hanging from his waist came in front of the thread-like reflection, it started melting.

'Move away,' Malphus screamed, pushing Jonathan away.

'Jesus!' Jonathan screamed, looking at his melted sword.

'It's very dangerous. Maintain distance,' Dimitri warned and started moving towards the bushes in which the reflection was going and some strange sound was coming.

Taking care of the dangerous thread reflection, Zoran ripped the bush away. In the bush, a crystal-like stone was slowly melting because of the reflection and something like a paper and key was in the middle of the crystal stone.

'It looks like a key and paper,' Malphus said, looking at the stone.

'The mystery on this mountain is much more than our expectation,' Theodore said, staring at the stone.

When the stone was half melted, the key and paper came out. Dimitri, moving slowly towards the half-melted crystal stone that was as hot as the sun, took the key and paper out.

On the top of the key, a dragon was made and the key was like the tail of a dragon. The paper was almost yellow and some numbers and a name at last were written on it.

978-3-5, 658-5-9, 876-9-16, 888-5-17, 323-6-19

Trevor Langford

'Trevor Langford,' Dmitri said surprisingly.

'Father,' Malphus asked.

'It looks like he wrote this piece of paper because his name is in the last,' Dimitri said.

Malphus snatched the piece of paper from Dimitri's hand.

'My father wrote this letter. It must be meant for something important, we need to find out. I knew my father would have left something to be found out by me. He knew that one day I will come on this mountain,' Malphus babbled.

'Calm down, calm down, Malphus. We will find out what your father wanted to convey to us,' Zoran said, holding Malphus.

'Yes, yes. I have seen the same symbol of dragon on the statue. It might be a key for that. Come with me,' Jonathan said, looking at the key.

They ran back to the statue from which the reflection was falling on the stone.

'Where is the symbol?' Malphus babbled.

'It was on the statue, I saw it,' Jonathan said, moving around the statue.

'It's here. It's here. Give me the key,' Malphus spluttered.

Malphus took they key and entered it into the hole in the statue and turned it to the left. The turning of the key made a creaking sound and the statue started moving towards the left and an entrance started opening at the

Saurabh Gupta

base of the statue. Due to the movement of the statue, the reflection of sunrays stopped.

'It's a trapdoor,' Zoran said.

When the statue was fully moved towards the left, the trapdoor was fully opened. It was pitch black inside the trapdoor.

'Everyone will not enter at once. We don't know what's inside it. Theodore, you light the flambeau and give it to me and follow me. Zoran, you stay here with Jonathan and Mendis,' Dimitri ordered.

Before Dimitri, Malphus entered into the trapdoor without any flambeau. Dimitri tried to stop him, but he just jumped into it. He was not able to control himself from what he was witnessing.

Taking the flambeau, Dimitri with Theodore entered inside. The trapdoor started with a number of stairs that ended onto a sandy base. Malphus was just in front of them. It was a very congested place with ceiling just five feet above which was causing problem for Theodore and Malphus.

As they moved further, they saw a skeleton lying on the ground.

'Someone was buried alive in this trapdoor,' Theodore said.

'He must be one of the adventurers, see the mark on his head. It was made on everybody who joined Sir Thomas on the journey,' Malphus said, touching the skeleton.

'But why was he buried alive?' Theodore said.

'Here is another one!' Dimitri shouted and Theodore and Malphus rushed towards him.

The second skeleton was holding an oval-shaped thing in his hand and was in a sitting position with his back on the wall.

'What's this in his hand?' Theodore said.

'He is Trevor Langford,' Dimitri said, looking at the ring in his pinky finger.

'Father,' Malphus said glumly, looking at the finger.

Malphus went speechless and was just staring at the skeleton of his father. He touched the ring and tears rolled out of his eyes.

Zoran, Mendis, and Jonathan were curiously waiting at the entrance of the trapdoor when Dimitri with the oval-shaped thing came out of it. Malphus's excitement while entering was all gone. He was coming out with a pale face, and Theodore was helping him to move out of the small cave.

'What is this, and what happened to Malphus?' Zoran blurted out.

'We found this and two skeletons inside the trapdoor. One was of an adventurer and another one was of Malphus's father,' Dimitri said coldly, handing the oval-shaped thing to Zoran.

Malphus came out of the trapdoor and went into the jungles. No one was having the heart to stop him. Everyone knew that he needs to be alone. Everyone knew what his father meant to him. It was not like he was not aware that his father was dead, but finding his skeleton inside the mysterious cave was on one side raising many questions and on another side was tickling Malphus's wound of loneliness. Jonathan and Mendis knew much more than anybody else how he was feeling.

A boy whose aim in life was to one day get on the mountain and kill a dragon who was responsible for his father's death was now lost again. On one side, Malphus was thinking what could have happened to his father, and on other side, he was looking at the piece of paper with the name of his father.

Near the statue, everyone was checking out the oval-shaped thing. According to Dimitri, it was a dragon's egg and Zoran was also thinking the same.

'If Malphus's father and an adventurer were there inside the statue, where is Sir Thomas's skeleton?' Jonathan asked.

'It might have so happened that Sir Thomas after handing over the egg to them went on to fight with the dragons,' Dimitri guessed.

'But why would he protect a dragon's egg from the dragons?' Mendis questioned.

'I think he wanted to take it away, but Sir Thomas was a noble man. He can't do this,' Zoran said.

'All the things are in the paper which is in Malphus's hand,' Dimitri said.

Just after a moment, Malphus came running towards the statue, and everyone was surprised with his excitement because the way he left, it was looking like he will not return till dawn.

'The book. This code is the page number, paragraph, and word. Give me my bag. The paper is coded according to the Book of Dragons written by Sir Thomas,' Malphus babbled.

'It looks like whoever left this message, the finger thing in the statue, wanted all these things to be revealed to someone from Riffsland because no one in the world knows about his sixth finger in his right hand and the Book of Dragons other than a citizen of Riffsland,' Zoran said.

'Here, here is the book,' Mendis said, handing over the book to Malphus.

Malphus, turning the pages frantically, started matching the pages, paragraphs, and words. Going through the pages, he was muttering something and finally he spoke.

'RETURN THE EGG TO DRAGONS AND—'

'And what?' Dimitri asked.

'That's it. The code ends with *and*. After that, my father's name is there,' Malphus said.

'It can't be possible, we are missing something,' Zoran said.

'The code ends here and nothing more is there,' Malphus miffed.

'We need to return the egg. That's what your father wanted,' Dimitri said.

'But if he wanted to return it, then from whom was he protecting it, and as far as I know, no one would bury himself alive,' Mendis asked.

'Sir Thomas.' Malphus made a wild guess.

'He was the only one other than your father and the other man,' Zoran supported Malphus.

'No, no. Sir Thomas can't do this. He was a great and noble man,' Dimitri sniffed.

'But he was crazy about dragons,' Zoran said.

'If returning the egg was what my father wanted then I will fulfill his dream' Malphus said.

'And in return, we will get the pick' Dimitri added.

'Do you think we can negotiate with these wild dragons?' Zoran disagreed.

'Do we have any other option?' Dimitri asked.

Zoran opened his mouth, swallowed, and then said, 'Okay, we will again go back to Thundering Mountain for the last time and will return with the Pick of Dragon,' Zoran said to everyone.

'Prepare your weapons and rope. We will swing to the Thundering Mountain and no one will be left on this side,' Dimitri said.

'It means we'll be going as well?' Mendis asked with bated breath.

'I think so,' Jonathan said.

Dimitri, respecting Malphus's values, gave the egg to him. They all tied the rope and were ready to swing to the Thundering Mountain for the second and last time. On one go, they all swung to the Thundering Mountain. Some fell on the ground and rolled down while some landed perfectly. The silence at the Thundering Mountain was the same as when Dimitri went there for the first time. But he knew that this silence is the invitation for upcoming waves.

'How to find the dragons?' Jonathan asked.

'They will find us,' Zoran said.

As expected, suddenly a huge wave of Ticklers came from the left. Dimitri, taking his hammer, jumped into the wave and shouted, 'Run to the middle, the pick must be at the middle of the mountain.'

Dimitri, rotating his hammer, passed by the first wave of Ticklers by smashing all the Ticklers that came in his way, but as he turned backwards, he saw a ten times bigger wave of Ticklers and shouted, 'Come on. I am gonna smash each one of you!' while others started running towards the middle of the mountain. The egg was with Malphus. Zoran's eyes were sharp and he suddenly saw a Bolt coming towards them. He took his arrow and fired it with the speed of light right into the head of the Bolt, which rolled down on the ground, passing just near to Jonathan who jumped onto it.

But this was not it. One after another, the Bolt started coming, and it was getting difficult for Zoran to fight with them while running with others.

'Take the egg with you. I am going to deal with these Bolts!' Zoran shouted and stopped at one place, with head down and looking at the ground.

All of a sudden, just in a second, he shot five Bolts. He took another arrow and fired it towards a tree. The arrow's tip was having numbers of pointed needles, which swell into the air and hit another four Bolts.

Leaving Zoran and Dimitri behind, Jonathan, Mendis, Malphus, and Theodore were still running like anything.

'Kneel down!' Theodore shouted and two Omnipotents passed with just an inch of air separating them.

They turned back and again started coming towards them. Theodore, trying to save Malphus, got lifted away by one of the Omnipotents and another one took Mendis in his grab.

'Mendis!' Jonathan squealed.

'We don't have time. Run, Jonathan, run,' Malphus said, pushing Jonathan up.

Now only Malphus with the egg and Jonathan were left. Running like anything, finally they reached at the middle of the mountain.

'There is no Pick of Dragon,' Jonathan spluttered.

'Don't forget about the Camouflaged dragons,' Malphus said.

They looked at every part of the area, but it looked like no dragons were there, but then Malphus's eyes stuck at the algae on a small cliff which was moving. Malphus moved slowly towards it, and suddenly a dragon swelled out of it and the egg fell from Malphus's hand.

The dragon had the same color as the mountain and suddenly three more dragons from the tree, branches, and bushes came out. It was looking like they were the masters of camouflage and they started moving slowly towards Malphus.

Malphus slowly took his mace out and shouted, 'Jonathan, the egg!'

Two of the dragons flew towards the egg while one attacked Malphus. Jonathan jumped onto the egg and suddenly he noticed a very thin dragon with a shining pick on his head hiding behind the trees.

'The dragon with the pick!' Jonathan shouted and Malphus turned towards him.

As Jonathan grabbed the egg and closed his eyes knowing that he will be killed by the two Camouflaged dragons, the small dragon, which saved Malphus, came from the sky and rammed the two dragons. Jonathan opened his eyes and saw the small dragon coming towards him, but he was coming for the egg. Malphus took the egg from Jonathan's hand and jumped into the bushes. The small dragon now ran towards Malphus with the egg.

On one side, Malphus was trying to hide from the small dragon, and on the other side, Jonathan ran towards the dragon with the pick who was trying to hide.

Malphus jumped out of the bushes with his mace and attacked the small dragon, but he dodged Malphus and, taking the egg in his mouth, flew away. But Malphus was not ready to leave him and caught his leg and flew away with him.

The small dragon, taking Malphus with him, flew far away from the middle of the mountain and landed on a barren field of the Thundering Mountain. Malphus rolled down on the ground and his piece of paper on which the code was written came out of his pocket and got hung upside down. But this time some more codes appeared on it.

Taking the piece of paper, Malphus hid into the bushes. He took out the book and started matching the codes. The Book of Dragon was in two parts, the second part of which appeared when the book was turned upside down, which Malphus did, and suddenly he mumbled, 'Oh no, the other half of the code was like the book. It appeared when turned upside down.'

He started matching the letters as fast as he could and spoke.

'AND TRY TO SAVE IT FROM.'

He then read the name of his father. Malphus was stunned. The letter was not written by his father, but it was written by someone else, trying to save it from his father, but then what about the ring in the finger of the skeleton?

As Malphus was paralyzed after reading the second part of the letter, the small dragon rammed him out of the bushes and the egg rolled down on the ground. The small dragon went flying towards the egg and engulfed it.

'No!' Malphus screamed, and all of a sudden, the small dragon's body started changing and he started howling.

It was looking like his whole body was shrinking. The flesh from the dragon's body was falling slowly and something was trying to come out of it. Malphus was stunned and stepped backwards, staring at the dragon. From the chest of the dragon, a human hand came out and finally a naked man appeared out of the falling pieces of fleshes covered in the blood and flesh of the dragon.

'F . . . Father,' Malphus mumbled.

It was Trevor Langford. He was holding the egg, which was now shining.

'Is that you?' Malphus asked.

'Son,' Langford croaked and hugged Malphus tightly.

'What has happened to you, Father?' Malphus sobbed.

'I do not have much time. Return this to the dragons.'

'But—'

'I will answer your every question, but first return it to the dragons,' Langford said and fell on the ground.

'Father,' Malphus sobbed.

'I said go,' Langford howled and Malphus ran towards the middle of the mountain.

At the middle of the mountain, all were surrounded by five giant Omnipotents. Zoran was holding the skinny dragon with the pick in his arms.

'Here is the egg. Take this and leave my friends!' Malphus shouted.

One of the Omnipotents saw the egg and hurtled towards Malphus, but all of a sudden, the egg moved. A leg came out of the egg by breaking it. It was a baby dragon. All the Omnipotents flew towards the baby dragon. One of them touched the baby dragon with his nose and then glared at Malphus. But then taking the baby dragon in his mouth, they flew away and the skinny dragon moved towards Jonathan and bowed down.

Jonathan, shivering, moved his hands towards the Pick of Dragon and took it away from the dragon's head. It looked like the skinny dragon knew that only Jonathan could take it out. Jonathan was not able to believe what he was holding. The pick was shining like gold and a mysterious dragon was drawn on it. Jonathan was feeling the power of the pick and his hands were still shivering. He was not even blinking his eyes and was continuously looking at the pick.

'The Pick of Dragon.' Jonathan sighed.

'My father,' Malphus mumbled and ran back. Everyone hearing the word *father* followed Malphus.

They reached to the barren part of the field where Trevor Langford was lying on the ground. Everyone got dazed after seeing him. Dimitri for a second went paralyzed. He was not able to believe what his eyes were seeing. Same was the case with others. A man who died with the legend Sir Thomas almost thirteen years ago was now lying on the ground alive.

'Father,' Malphus sobbed, taking his father into his lap.

'Sir Langford, you are alive. Then the skeleton with your ring inside the underground chamber was of . . .,' Dimitri exclaimed, coming closer to Langford.

'That must be Sir Thomas. I gave him the ring in the start of our journey as a symbol of luck. When we came to this mountain, our number started decreasing due to the attack by the dragons. When others were busy in learning about dragons, I was in the search of becoming like one of them and what I needed was a bath with dragon's blood in full moonlight with other herbs, bones, and a dragon's egg, but Sir Thomas was against it and he got to know about the egg which I stole from the dragons. The egg which I stole was of the lady dragon that was considered as a blessing for other dragons. That was the reason why they were attacking us. But till that time I went mad. I performed all the rituals under full moonlight, but when I searched for the egg, it was gone. It was taken away by Sir Thomas. I didn't know that if all the rituals will be performed without the egg, one will be cursed and turned into the rejected species of dragon, and every night, he will suffer the pain of death. Sir Thomas hid himself inside the statue with one of his disciples and sacrificed his life for saving the egg. I became a cursed dragon and I wanted to correct all the things by engulfing the egg again and giving it life by sacrificing mine,' Langford faltered.

'No, Father, I will not let you go,' Malphus sobbed.

'I have got the punishment for my sins and the remaining will be given to me in hell,' Langford said and his eyes closed.

'Father,' Malphus howled and everyone bowed down not for the Sir Langford who stole the egg, but for the man who decided to live with the curse and pass every night with the pain of death just to return the egg and make things correct for others.

They got the Pick of Dragon, and the mystery of Sir Thomas and Sir Langford was solved, but Malphus decided to stay at the Thundering Mountain and serve the dragons for the rest of his life. The thing for which his father sacrificed his life, he wanted to carry it on and pay the debts left. Now with only five left, the travelers moved down from the Thundering Mountain towards the String of Snakes.

CHAPTER EIGHTEEN

STRING OF SNAKES

They were all moving afoot and were missing their horses. According to the Red Paper, between the String of Snakes and the land, there existed a big ocean. The String of Snakes was on an island named Milosa. No one from Riffsland knew about it. Earlier the Thundering Mountain was also far beyond their reach like the island Milosa, but with hope and belief in themselves, they were able to get the Buried Belt and the Pick of Dragon.

They were moving in a jungle in the daylight and which was not ready to end. The jungle started from the Thundering Mountain and was still going.

'I can't understand why Theodore is keeping all the two powers. You are the one who took the powers. You are the one who was able to take it out, then why the hell he is keeping it with him,' Mendis complaint.

'He is the son of Sir Andrew Blake. In his veins run the blood of the greatest guitarist in this universe. The Blood Shredder is not a cakewalk. Its powers are beyond my control. Theodore is the deserving one and he will get it. I did it because I wanted to know the reality and you did it for our friendship. This is it. After this journey, we will get back to our homes and will never reveal the secret of Riffsland.'

'But then can you tell me why were you able to get near the Blood Shredder, convert the guard's instrument into a weapon, get the Buried Belt and Pick of Dragon, and why were you the one to whom the story of Riffsland was being told as a folklore throughout his life,' Mendis fired questions one upon another.

'I don't know and even they don't know. To find what's special about me or why I am able to do these things, I came to this journey, and even if I return without any revelation, I will give my hundred percent to what I have committed.'

'I heard it from Dimitri that the String of Snakes is on an island Milosa. Do you have any idea how we can pass the ocean?'

'Dimitri and Zoran must be having something in their minds. We don't have to think about that,' Jonathan said.

'Malphus must be very happy on the Thundering Mountain. He got what he wanted to. But it would be very difficult for him to get friendly with those dreadful dragons. The Omnipotents, Bolt, and others, all were unique and dangerous.' Mendis sighed.

'He returned the egg to them which they were searching from thirteen years and I think the dragons will not forget his face, and when he will get near those dragons, they will recognize him for sure.'

'Hope so.'

The long jungle was about to end and the sound of the ocean was coming closer. They had no idea how to cross the ocean, how to deal with snakes, and who else will be there on the island.

Zoran chopped the big leaves that were obstructing the view of the ocean. There he saw what was least expected at such a deserted and isolated area. Near the ocean, there existed a village. There were number of houses made of wood and smoke was coming out from most of the chimneys of the houses. Not only the houses but most of the things were made of wood like the carts, wheels, chimney, tables, and shoes lying on the ground, armory, and other things. But there was no sign of the ones who lived there. But looking at the smoke and undone work, they knew that someone will come soon. There were a number of wood cutters and all the things related to carpenters. Calling this a village of carpenters was not wrong anyway.

'A village,' Dimitri said.

'This is strange. Life also exists at such an isolated area,' Zoran added.

'We must go and check,' Theodore exclaimed.

'Stop, stop. Someone is coming,' Dimitri whispered.

From the jungles there came a group of the villagers. They were carrying lots of wood with them. They were of average height with long ears and most of them were skinny. All of them wore golden bangles on their hands.

'Who are they?' Theodore asked.

'They are the Wooders. They live in isolated areas. I thought their species was vanished by the Guttadevers. They are the finest carpenters in the world and they work for precious stones only. If you pay them stones, they will work for you,' Zoran said.

'It means they can make boats for us?' Mendis asked.

'Only they can,' Zoran said.

'Then we must go and deal with them,' Jonathan said.

'They are very sensitive. Just one wrong move and they will kill you on the spot. No one knows why they are living here and why they have been underground for so many years, and relation between Riffsland and the Wooders had not been much good,' Dimitri said.

The group of Wooders came into the village and one of them ranged the bell hanging. Hearing the bell, Wooders from every house started coming out. The village that was looking deserted just a second ago was now filled with Wooders and looked much active. Some of them started taking out the woods, while some of them passed them to the machine for being cut down.

'Let's go and no one will speak a single word,' Dimitri ordered and they started moving towards the village.

Seeing them, all the Wooders were surprised, but from their expression, it was difficult to guess whether they were just staring or glaring. All the Wooders stopped their work and started moving towards them.

Dimitri tightened the grip on his hammer and was ready to act on any reaction from the Wooders, but from the bunch of Wooders, there came another one who was dressed blue with blue lines on his cheek.

'Musicians,' the one chuckled.

'I, Dimitri, the adviser of The Three and leader of the Nimbler family, pay warm regards to the Wooders,' Dimitri said politely.

'So much of abdicate. You musicians are just a toy of war. These things don't suit you. Oh, a white whisperer this far from Riffsland. This is not a safe place for you. Others are hungry for your blood.'

Hearing this, the whisperer hid behind Mendis.

'We are here to eliminate the rise of evils,' Zoran said.

'I don't talk to musicians,' the Wooder thundered, hearing which Zoran stepped towards him, but Dimitri stopped him.

'We are here for the String of Snakes,' Dimitri said.

'So that you can again start a war which will end hundreds of tribes like us. We faced the consequences of war without any involvement and you enjoyed getting back to your kingdom after the war. Those evils were a product of your kingdom and training.'

'We are also on the side of peace and to minimize the chances of the rise of evil. We need to get the String of Snakes so that we can bring back the most powerful instrument, and if it gets into the hands of evil, it will kill more than hundreds of tribes for sure.'

'And what do you want from us?'

'We want you to make a boat for us.'

'And the stones?'

'We have them,' Dimitri said and took out a pouch from his pocket.

'The stones! You musicians are very good at it. This will be enough for a single boat,' the Wooder said, taking the stones from Dimitri.

'How long will it take?' Dimitri asked.

'Time is not of much importance here for the Wooders and specially for making things out of wood and it would be better if you don't ask about it again,' the Wooder growled.

The leader of the Wooders, who took the stones from Dimitri's hand, signaled the others to start the work. They

259

took the big trunk, which they must have chopped minutes ago, and passed it through the cutter. After the cutter, they started shaping the pieces of trunk into different parts of boats. They were born to be carpenters and really good carpenters. Anything made from wood in the whole world was available in the village of Wooders.

'Why does he hate musicians?' Mendis asked.

'Before the darkest night, they used to sell their products to many including Riffsland, but the war pierced deeper within them which, I think, forced them to move away from the center and get settled in a deserted area, away from any musician or other living beings. Looking at the village, I guess that now they make products for their own use and they learnt the technique of hunting and killing to survive without selling and getting stones, but still their love for stones remains the same. It was their weakness. They'll start working for anyone who offers them stones,' Dimitri said.

'Looks like the war has affected them a lot,' Jonathan said, sitting on the ground.

'It has made them hunters and rivals of musicians,' Dimitri said.

'But they hate debt more than any musician in the world,' Zoran said.

'Debt! What do you mean?' Mendis asked.

'They ask the right price for whatever they give, and if they get more than that, they pay it back with interest. Once their ancestor almost destroyed the tribe by taking huge debts which he failed to pay. They were made slaves and were forced to work until the debt was paid. After getting free from the slavery of almost thirty years, they took the oath of not taking any debt, and if taken by mistake or in crucial circumstances, they will pay it back with interest as soon as possible,' Zoran said.

'It is good for us,' Mendis said and took the whisperer on his shoulder.

'Don't you think, Dimitri, that the dragon carved on the Pick of Dragon is very strange and I don't think that we have seen any dragon like this on the Thundering Mountain,' Theodore asked, looking at the Pick of Dragon.

'Let me see,' Dimitri asked for the pick.

'The dragon carved on the pick is, you can say, a mix of all dragons. He is called as the ancestor of all dragons, but no one has ever seen him. He exists as a force which one can only feel,' Dimitri said.

The Wooders didn't take much time to make the boat. The boat was made with a perfect finishing touch. It was big enough for five people and was even carved with beautiful flowers, branches, and the symbol of the Wooders with wooden planks and axe at both side and a jungle at the middle.

'This is really nice,' Jonathan exclaimed.

'Looks like we got much more than what we have paid,' Mendis said, getting into the boat.

'So your boat is ready. This is what we can give you in return of the stones you gave,' the Wooder said.

'Thank you for your contribution in our attempt to wipe evil off the face of this planet,' Dimitri uttered.

'We are ready to go,' Zoran said, pushing the boat towards the ocean.

Dimitri shook hands with the Wooder who didn't fancy speaking to any musician and ran towards the boat. He jumped into the boat in which the others were already sitting. Giving the final push, Zoran also jumped into the boat.

The ocean was really big, and far across the ocean, there was no sign of any island. Looking at the ocean, it seemed like even if they sail for a year, they will not find anything else. There were two rafts attached to the board, one on the left side and another one on the right side. Mendis and Jonathan were on the raft. The ocean was still, which might be because it was daytime. According to Dimitri, the island was almost a day away, which meant that they would have to spend the night on the boat. The ocean, according to Zoran, was always dangerous at night with a number of monsters inside the ocean who move out of their caves deep inside the ocean for hunting.

They took some fruits from the jungle to eat and were having only one pouch of fresh drinking water. Dimitri warned everyone to drink it only when needed because he said that dying of water shortage is the ugliest of deaths in the ocean.

Jonathan and Mendis were exhausted and now the turn was of Theodore and Dimitri to take control of the raft. It was dawn, and by drinking just a little from the pouch of freshwater, Jonathan and Mendis fell on the boat and fell asleep.

Jonathan saw that his mom and dad were standing in front of him and suddenly he started falling into a big well, which was endless; he kept falling into the well and his dad started screaming, 'Jonathan, Jonathan!'

Jonathan suddenly opened his eyes and saw Mendis waking him up by calling his name. It was all dark and the stars were glittering with the moon hiding behind the clouds. He was on the boat and everyone was mum.

'Hshhhhh, the monsters are near,' Mendis whispered.

'Monsters,' Jonathan mumbled.

'Looks like you had a nightmare,' Mendis whispered.

Jonathan crawled to the edge of the boat to see what was there inside the ocean. It was all dark and nothing was visible. Dimitri, Zoran, and Theodore were all looking below the boat into the ocean. The pin-drop silence was making the situation more blood-curdling. An endless ocean at night in which nothing was visible and a suspicious monster just below the boat was the worst situation.

Suddenly someone rammed the boat from the bottom.

'Something is there,' Mendis shouted.

'Shut your mouth,' Dimitri snarled.

Again something rammed the boat heavily, which made Jonathan fall on the base of the boat.

'Hold something,' Zoran shouted.

'Smell of the fruits. He is coming because of that,' Dimitri said.

'We can't throw them, it is all what we are left with to eat,' Mendis said and the whisperer jumped off from his shoulder.

'Don't be childish. Throw all of them including the chocolates which you feed to your whisperer,' Zoran growled.

Mendis, looking at the whisperer, took the fruits and chocolates and wrapped them into his coat.

The ramming started frequently and much more heavily this time. Everyone was holding the boat and no one was able to stand due to the ramming.

'Throw them as much far as you can,' Dimitri shouted.

Mendis, rotating the fruits and chocolates wrapped in his coat, threw it as far as he could, and as it fell in the ocean, something out of the dark came out and engulfed it.

'What took you so long to throw the food? We could have been killed by that monster just because of you,' Theodore thundered.

'Calm yourself, boy, he is gone,' Dimitri said to Theodore.

'Sorry, whisperer,' Mendis apologized and the whisperer hugged his leg.

'He was big,' Jonathan said, looking into the ocean.

'There are many like him under the water,' Zoran said.

'It's better if we keep mum for the rest of our journey because noise and food attracts them,' Dimitri said.

'Don't worry, we will not die of hunger,' Zoran said, looking at the miserable faces of Mendis and the whisperer.

'We will get something to eat on the island,' Dimitri said.

'Is he gone?' Jonathan mumbled.

'Yes,' Zoran said.

'Zoran and Jonathan, go and take the control of the raft, the island must not be very far from here,' Dimitri said, looking into the endless darkness of the ocean.

It was Jonathan who woke up first on the boat. The sky was clear, ocean was still, and the awful night was gone. An island was in front of them, but still too far. Seeing the island, Jonathan shouted, 'The island, the island, it's here!'

Rubbing his eyes, Mendis said, 'Which island?'

'The Island of Snakes,' Jonathan exclaimed.

By that time, everyone woke up and Jonathan was right, it was the Island of Snakes in front of them.

'Our last destination,' Dimitri said.

'No musician has ever stepped onto that island before. We are the first ones,' Zoran added.

The boat touched the island. After just fifteen to twenty steps, there started a dense forest on the island that was all dark. Dimitri stepped onto the island first, followed by the others.

'I thought each inch of this island would be filled with snakes, but it's not like that,' Mendis said, taking the whisperer onto his shoulder.

'It's so silent here,' Zoran said.

'The story of snakes can also be a myth,' Jonathan said.

'Three of us would stay near the boat and the rest two will go into the jungle because we can't afford to lose our boat. It's our only way of getting away,' Dimitri said.

'Theodore, Jonathan, and Mendis, stay near the boat and don't enter the forest until we signal you,' Zoran said.

Dimitri and Zoran entered into the jungle. The island was quite silent, which was not expected after listening to the things which they heard about it. After throwing the chocolates and other eating items, they all were quite hungry.

'Let me check if there is something to eat on this island or not,' Theodore said.

'But don't enter into the forest,' Jonathan said, but Theodore ignored and moved towards the forest.

As Theodore was just about to enter into the forest, Dimitri came out of it. He was looking in hurry and was panting.

'Come fast, follow me,' Dimitri said and again went into the jungle without waiting for others to come.

'What was that?' Theodore mumbled.

Jonathan came running from behind and pushed Theodore with him to follow Dimitri before he gets out of sight.

Jonathan, Mendis, and Theodore entered into the jungle, but Dimitri was not there. Instead of the bright sunshine outside, the jungle was dark.

'Dimitri!' Jonathan shouted, looking at each possible direction.

'Where are you?' Theodore squealed and then someone shouted.

'Hurry, follow me!'

Jonathan looked towards the right and saw Dimitri running into the jungle. It was looking like Dimitri was in a hurry and seeing him without Zoran was making things much more confusing.

'Is he testing us?' Mendis said while running.

'I don't know. Just follow him,' Jonathan replied.

After following him for just some seconds, he again got lost.

'Dimitri!' Mendis shouted.

'Don't run so fast, and for god's sake, stop hiding,' Theodore squealed.

'There. There he is,' Jonathan said in alarm.

They again got a glimpse of Dimitri running much deeper into the jungle and this hide-and-seek kept going until they reached an old temple-like structure at the middle of the forest, and as usual, Dimitri again got vanished.

'What the hell is this?' Theodore said, looking at the temple.

'We are in the middle of the forest and still we haven't even seen a single snake or any living creature. A forest without any animals is weird,' Mendis said.

They again saw Dimitri opening the door of the trapdoor and signaling them to enter. Without wasting a single second, they all entered into the pitch-dark trapdoor. Touching the walls, they slowly started going down, and all of a sudden, Mendis lost his balance, and taking Jonathan and Theodore with him, he rolled down to the ground.

'Move away from me,' Theodore miffed.

'Jonathan!' someone called from the dark.

'Zoran,' Theodore made a guess.

'Here, here. I am here,' Zoran said.

Following the sound, Theodore reached near Zoran and touched him. Theodore was not able to guess where his legs, hands, or head were.

'Take the pick out of my pocket,' Zoran said.

As Theodore took the pick out and rubbed them, his leg got trapped, and all of a sudden, he got hung upside down. Same happened with Jonathan and Mendis, but the whisperer fell on the ground. The pick that Theodore was rubbing fell on the ground and started glowing.

Now everything was visible. In a row, Jonathan, Mendis, Theodore, Zoran, and even Dimitri were hanging upside down. Seeing Dimitri hanging upside down and unconscious was the most strange thing for Jonathan,

Mendis, and Theodore because he was the one who took them there and now he was hanging like a dead body.

'Dimitri,' Theodore was surprised.

'Yes. While getting trapped, his head banged the wall and he fainted,' Zoran said with difficulty as he was hanging upside down and all the blood was pumping to his head.

'Wait a second. From how long is he hanging here?' Jonathan asked.

'From the moment you all entered the forest, going against our order, and God knows why you came to this underground passage and we followed you till here and you all got vanished and we got trapped,' Zoran said.

'We entered into the jungle and you followed us?' Jonathan said in alarm.

'Yes, I said the same,' Zoran said.

'Dimitri called us into the jungle and we followed him till here and now you are telling us that you guys followed us?' Theodoroe said.

'Wait a second. If neither you nor we asked to follow, then who did?' Zoran said.

'No, no. This is not possible. I saw myself that Dimitri was leading us, and yes, he was acting weird, but he was Dimitri,' Mendis said.

'Hey, whisperer, untie us,' Jonathan said and the whisperer jumped to hold the rope, but the rope was a little high from his reach and there was nothing to climb upon.

'We'll discuss later who followed whom. First, we need to get out of this trap,' Zoran said and Dimitri made some movement.

'See, Dimitri is waking,' Mendis exclaimed.

'Oh my head! It's throbbing!' Dimitri howled.

'You asked them to follow us?' Zoran asked.

'Who asked to follow who, and why the hell are we hanging upside down?' Dimitri said.

'Because we came here following these kids and now they're saying they came here following us,' Zoran puzzled.

'What the hell,' Dimitri miffed.

'Hshhhh . . . Something is coming,' Zoran said.

The sound was coming from the entrance of the underground passage. It sounded like something was entering into the underground passage and it was for sure great in number. It was sounding like waves floating as slow as possible, and all of a sudden, everything became silent. The whisperer jumped onto a rock.

'What was that?' Jonathan said.

Suddenly a small snake fell into the ground. It was very small and yellow in color with black spots. It wasn't looking dangerous and was slithering on the ground. The whisperer came back on the ground and held the small snake by its tail and suddenly a huge number of different snakes flooded into the underground passage. Seeing the wave, the whisperer jumped onto the highest rock and now the room was full of snakes. They all were different. Some were small, some were big, and some were just unexplainable. The flood of snakes constituted of rattlesnakes, black mamba, cobra, anaconda, cottonmouth, and many others. The sound of hissing was filling the room, and hanging upside down in such a situation was not making things better. One of the snakes, who was very small, jumped towards Mendis, and just when his teeth were about to reach Mendis's nose, he fell back on the ground.

'He was going to kill me,' Mendis screamed.

'Try to be away from the ground as much as you can,' Dimitri said.

'How the hell did this happen? We came crossing the whole forest and didn't see any single animal and now the ground of this underground room is filled with a variety of snakes,' Jonathan said.

'We are on the Island of Snakes and it was expected,' Zoran said.

Again two snakes jumped from the ground and fell, reaching just near to Jonathan and Mendis.

'We will not be able to survive like this. Not for long,' Theodore screamed.

'He is coming,' Mendis screamed, showing his finger towards a snake slithering on the walls.

'Zoran, try to get the knife from my pocket. I haven't put a knot on it,' Dimitri said.

Zoran started swinging himself towards Dimitri. He failed on the first try, but on second try, he missed it just by an inch. Going back this time, he pushed himself as far as he could and finally reached the knife. Holding the knife, first he cut Dimitri's rope and then his own. Swinging with the help of the rope, Dimitri jumped onto a piece of rock while Zoran was still cutting ropes.

'Here is a way,' Dimitri shouted, signaling towards a big hole into the wall.

Taking the whisperer onto his shoulder, Dimitri entered into the hole. After cutting everyone's rope, all of them entered into the hole. Entering into the hole, for the last time, Mendis looked back at the flood of snakes, hissing and still hungry for their blood and eager to either inject their venom or crush their bones.

They all came out of the hole that led them to the ground and were now in the middle of the jungle.

'Who was missing snakes?' Zoran shouted.

'But there were too many,' Mendis said.

'No, I don't think so,' Jonathan said, looking towards the jungle.

Everyone turned into the direction where Jonathan was looking and what they saw paralyzed them for a moment. The number of snakes in the underground passage was now looking like a glimpse of what they were seeing now. From the jungle, covering the whole land and the trees, a humongous flood of numerous snakes were swelling towards them. Due to the movement of those snakes, the ground was even shaking.

'Run towards the mountains in the middle,' Dimitri shouted and everyone started running towards the mountain, which was at the middle of the island.

Seeing back while running was just like a nightmare and the flood was coming closer and closer. The mountain was still looking far maybe because of the dense forest. They were running like anything and the flood was following them like a shadow but with increasing speed. It was looking like the snakes were passing by everything, the stones, trees, and whatever was coming in their way.

As the dense forest got clearer, they saw a dead end. The mountain was not a hope but a dead end for all of them. The mountain was standing at a 90-degree angle, which was impossible to climb. Mendis, petrified, started climbing the mountain but wasn't able to climb a single inch. The mountain was sharp and slippery. The sound of the flood of snakes started swelling. Jonathan held Dimitri tightly and so did the whisperer with Mendis. Zoran took out his bow and arrow and was still ready to fight.

The flood came out of the jungle, which almost covered the sky, and fell upon them. But the wave passed through them and then the mountains and disappeared like a ghost. Mendis was seeing snakes passing through him like ghosts and everyone was shocked.

'Where did they go?' Theodore said.

'Were they a mirage?' Jonathan guessed.

'Just like our duplicates that made us follow you to the underground passage,' Zoran said.

'It means whatever Jonathan guessed about the island was right. There are no snakes on this island. They were all a mirage,' Dimitri said.

'No, this can't be possible. I felt some snakes on my hand,' Jonathan said.

'Me too,' Theodore added.

'It might be possible that some were real out of them,' Dimitri said.

'Dimitri, look, three of them are there,' Mendis shouted.

'Follow them,' Zoran shouted.

The snakes were moving very fast and it was becoming difficult for them to keep an eye on the snakes. The three snakes of white, blue, and red color were moving alongside the mountain. Following the snakes, the mountain passed by, and just after the end of the mountain, there was a very old structure looking like another temple. The three snakes entered into the dark entrance of the temple.

'Was this jungle a holy place? There are so many temples!' Jonathan said.

'Are we going to follow them?' Mendis asked suspiciously.

'We don't have any other option,' Zoran said and they started moving towards the gate of the temple.

The entrance was not much dark. The sunlight coming from the cracks in the wall was making the passage visible. Although the temple was much old, still it was looking very strong, and apart from the cracks, the temple was strong enough to survive another decade.

'Where are they headed?' Theodore asked.

'It's a single path from here. We should just follow this path,' Dimitri said.

They entered into the passage. The walls of the temple were covered with algae and roots. The floor of the passage was a bed of dead leaves and branches.

Following the single path, they reached a point from where two ways were leading and both were looking identical.

'Which way?' Jonathan asked and suddenly everything started shaking and the sound of something coming very fast started swelling.

'What's that?' Mendis asked and looked towards the right and saw a huge wave of water coming like a giant to engulf them all.

'Run!' Dimitri shouted, and without thinking for a second, they started running towards the opposite side. The wave was huge and was looking very dreadful, the sound of which was making them frightened.

Water drops from the wave started falling upon them, which was a signal that they will be soon engulfed by it. Suddenly they saw two ways, one in the left and another in the right, which were their only hope of getting away from this gigantic wave.

They did not have much time to discuss who will jump where, so Dimitri and Zoran jumped to the right, Jonathan and Theodore to the left, but because of the slippery floor, Mendis failed to jump on any side and the waves was over his head to engulf him. Mendis, holding the whisperer tightly, closed his eyes. The sound swelling to its maximum limit passed through Mendis, just like the waves of snakes did.

Dimitri and Zoran, slipping through the hole in the right, fell into a hallway, while Jonathan and Theodore fell into a room.

'Did Mendis jumped?' Dimitri asked.

'I doubt that,' Zoran said.

Suddenly Jonathan came into the room and said, 'Are you all safe? We need to find Mendis!'

'Where is Mendis?' Zoran asked.

'I know, come follow me,' Jonathan said and Dimitri moved to follow him, but Zoran, taking his small knife, took a sharp shot on Jonathan and he vanished like a smoke.

'What was that?' Dimitri asked surprisingly.

'The water was also a hoax,' Zoran mumbled.

'What?'

'Yes. There is someone trying to keep us away from the String of Snakes.'

'How can you be so sure?'

'The wave of snakes, water, and these misleading characters of Jonathan, Theodore, and all those who are not with us signal to the same point.'

'And if we find him, we will be able to find the String of Snakes.'

'Yes.'

'But others don't know about it and it can turn into a disaster.'

'We need to find them,' Zoran said and they stepped towards the gate.

On the other side, Mendis with his whisperer also understood the hoax of all those things but only up to a limit. Mendis with his whisperer were having only one way to move forward and he started moving to that direction, while Jonathan and Theodore were also moving towards the center of the temple, which was through the down-going stairs.

'The snakes, two of them,' Theodore shouted, seeing the snakes passing by down on the ground.

'Hurry,' Jonathan said and ran behind the snakes.

'What if these both snakes are also a mirage?' Theodore said while running.

'Only one way to know it,' Jonathan said and Theodore understood.

Theodore took a small knife from his pocket and aimed at one of the snakes. While running, he was waiting for the right aim and finally he got it. He made a sharp throw and it hit the head of the snake and blood poured out of its head.

'He is real,' Jonathan panted, stopping at the dead snake with knife speared through his head.

'His flesh is vaporizing,' Theodore said.

The flesh of the snake started vaporizing like water does from a hot frying pan. As the whole snake vaporized, a string came out of it.

'What's this?' Jonathan kneeled down to take a closer look.

'It's a string,' Theodore said.

'It's the D string of a guitar,' Jonathan said and looked at Theodore. Both went speechless and were just looking at each other.

'It means the other strings are also the snakes,' Jonathan exclaimed.

'We need to find the other five snakes.'

'Yes, but we need to find others also and tell them about it.'

'Let's go.'

Mendis was not able to find anyone and was still running in the only single pathway and suddenly he stepped onto a broken piece of floor and some part of the floor fell with Mendis into a big cave beneath the temple.

The cave was huge and someone was sitting at the center of it. There was also a small waterfall in the cave. Apart from the sound of the falling water, the cave was numb. The ceiling of the cave was full of hanging pin-pointed rocks.

'Who's there?' Mendis shouted, looking at the person sitting at the center.

'They killed. They have killed one of my sons. They have killed a snake,' the one sitting at the center said calmly.

'Who are you?' Mendis said, moving towards the one.

'They don't treat them as one of their own. They will have to pay for it. I, the Mislead, will make them pay for killing my son.'

'Is this temple yours? We are searching for the snakes and some of the snakes entered in this temple and I lost the path.'

'You, you are one of them. If you will suffer, they will follow, just like I did.'

Mendis was finally able to see the one calling himself as Mislead. He was a very old man with small white beard and was very skinny and was wrapped in a thick piece of brown cloth. One of his eyes was white and other was black. There was also a mole on his nose, a big mole on his big nose. He was holding a stick in his hand on which the skin of snake was carved.

'You are the one who made the hoax of snakes and water waves,' Mendis said and suddenly roots emerged out of the ground and wrapped around his leg.

As the Mislead twisted his stick, the roots around Mendis's leg also clenched. The whisperer jumped off from Mendis's shoulder and started pulling the roots out of his leg.

'Hoax is what you saw outside, but this home of mine which some people call as cave is the real source of power. Playing and killing with my snakes is the last thing anyone in the world would think to do,' Mislead said.

'My friends will be coming soon,' Mendis howled.

'Ah! That's what I want because one of the six has been taken, but they will not be able to take it away from this temple.'

'What one of the six?'

'The strings which when I got, I thought I got everything, but the powers of it were restricted to this cave only, and outside it, I was able to create only mirages. So I sacrificed my freedom for this power. All those who come to this island run back just by the hoax and the remaining die here. Those six snakes are just like my sons, and a father, on the death of his son, can do anything for revenge.'

On the other side, Dimitri and Zoran, just following a path on luck, saw Jonathan again, running with Theodore.

'Dimitri!' Jonathan shouted, seeing Dimitri with Zoran.

Dimitri again took his small knife and threw it towards Jonathan who dodged it, and the knife passed by touching Jonathan, which made him bleed.

'Have you gone mad?' Theodore shouted on Dimitri.

'You are the real one,' Dimitri said, picking up Jonathan.

'What do you mean the real one?' Jonathan asked.

'Someone is making mirages of us to protect the string,' Zoran said.

'The string is in the snakes,' Jonathan said.

'What?' Dimitri said in alarm.

'See, we killed one of those snakes entering into the cave and we got the D string,' Jonathan explained.

'It means we need to find the five other snakes. I mean strings,' Zoran said.

'But we need to find Mendis first,' Jonathan reminded them.

'He was lost in the flood,' Theodore said.

'The mirage of flood,' Dimitri corrected him.

'The other two snakes,' Jonathan shouted.

'Zoran,' Dimitri said and Zoran with a single shot of his arrow killed both of the snakes.

One of the snakes started vaporizing and turned into an A string. Dimitri took the string in his hand.

'This does not look like the String of Snakes. It looks incomplete,' Dimitri doubted.

'Maybe by bringing all the strings together, it will turn to the original shape and size,' Zoran guessed.

'Now we need to find the other four strings and Mendis, but no one will go separately now. All of us will go together,' Dimitri said.

'Hshhhh, listen to the hissing,' Jonathan whispered.

'There are too many,' Theodore said, guessing on the hissing coming from the front way.

'But the main ones will only be three,' Dimitri said.

'And what if more than three are real?' Jonathan said.

'We don't have much option,' Dimitri said, and from every side, snakes started passing by.

From everywhere, the snakes were passing by and it was looking like none of them are real. They started killing as many as they can, but the flow of snakes was looking endless.

'They are all over,' Jonathan said.

'Kill them all but stay close,' Dimitri shouted.

All of them after being hit vanished like smoke and it was looking all the snakes were mirage.

One after another but none of them was turning into a string. They were keeping their eyes focused and aim sharp.

'This can go on for the whole day,' Jonathan panted.

'They are not decreasing and none of them are real,' Theodore said, and suddenly he felt a snake passing by his leg. Turning backwards with lighting speed, he shoved his knife into the snake, which started bleeding.

'I got one,' Theodore shouted and the snake turned into high E string, which was rusted like the other strings.

'The snake with two mouths,' Zoran shouted, and as it came near Dimitri, he slammed it under his hammer and the two-mouthed snake got squeezed under it, and as it died, all the other fake snakes disappeared.

'These are the other two strings but rusted. Now we need the last string, which is the G string,' Dimitri said, picking up the two strings.

'Dmitri!' someone howled.

'It's Mendis,' Jonathan said.

'Run!' Dimitri said, putting all the five strings in his pocket.

Following the sound, they reached near the other side of the waterfall.

'The sound is coming from behind this waterfall,' Jonathan said, and passing by the waterfall, they entered into the huge cave in which Mendis and the whisperer were tied with roots on the wall.

'Mendis!' Jonthan said and ran towards him, but suddenly a mace, entering into his shoulder, pinched him onto the wall and Jonathan growled with pain.

The Mislead came out of the darkness.

'You are the one,' Theodore thundered and ran towards him. Dimitri tried to stop, but he escaped, and as the Mislead turned his stick upwards, a huge piece of bamboo coming out from the ground hooked Theodore into the air and his guitar fell on the ground.

'Looks like you two are decent enough to talk,' the Mislead said.

'What do you want?' Dimitri asked.

'My five strings which you have taken because they are useless for you without the G string and a little revenge for killing my five sons.'

'So you are the one who has made this a fake Island of Snakes which is nothing more than a mirage,' Zoran said.

'Yes! Only the lucky ones come here and they see the flood of snakes and run away. No one ever has come so close to me. Some have also come to this temple, but none of them have reached my home which some people call cave.'

'Why can't we find the G string?' Zoran asked.

'Do I look like a fool? The thing which one hides is the thing which one does not want to tell, and you all will pay for killing my five sons.'

Dimitri looked at the right hand of the Mislead, which was sometimes shining like the skin of snakes. He took out the other five strings out and again the skin of the snake blinked for a fraction of second on his right hand.

'Here, take the five strings and leave them all,' Dimitri said politely, taking out the other five strings from his pocket.

'No, Dimitri. We haven't come so far to lose to this ugly fool,' Theodore howled and suddenly some roots coming out of the bamboo clenched around his neck.

'Don't call me fool again,' the Mislead said.

'Leave the child alone. I am giving you the strings,' Dimitri said.

'Come closer,' the Mislead said and Dimitri started moving towards him.

Dimitri, looking at Theodore and the others, gave the other strings to the Mislead.

'Now let them go,' Dimitri said.

'But what about the pain I have suffered? What about the pain which I suffered due to the loss of my children? I took care of them like my own sons. They came in my hands when they were very small. I have sacrificed everything and now you have killed all of them. You will have to pay for it,' the Mislead said and he moved to turn his stick.

Dimitri shouted, 'Now!' and Zoran threw the Pick of Dragon and Buried Belt towards the Mislead.

As the Mislead turned his stick, spikes started coming out of the ground, but before it could pierce Dimitri and Zoran, the Buried Belt and Pick of Dragon touched the five strings and they all produced a shining white light with huge force that threw them all away.

Holding his head, Zoran tried to see what happened. Theodore was lying on the ground. Mendis and the whisperer were out of root and Jonathan was trying to get up by holding his bleeding shoulder. As Zoran turned backwards, he saw the Mislead lying on the side, badly burnt, and was almost dead with just countable breath left.

Crawling towards the Mislead, Dimitri stood up in front of him.

'You were powerful, but when the three powers came in contact after a decade, they produced an uncontrollable energy, and since you have somehow injected the G string into your right hand, you were burnt, my dear friend Mislead,' Dimitri said and the Mislead was just looking at him. He was unable to speak a word or move any part of his body.

'Rest in peace,' Dimitri said and sliced the sword through his right hand, which fell apart and started vaporizing, which finally turned into the last G string. Mislead's eyes finally closed after the last moment of pain.

Dimitri, taking out the other five strings, touched it with the last string, and they all turned just like the skin of snakes and started shining brightly. Zoran, seeing all the strings, came closer to Dimitri and took them in his hand. He touched the strings lightly and spluttered, 'The String of Snakes.'

Mendis just heard the words that Zoran said and opened his hands to feel the energy of the strings from distance. The whisperer was trying to wake up Mendis. Jonathan, after seeing the String of Snakes together, smiled and fell back due to the pain in his shoulder. Theodore came running towards Zoran to just take a look at the finest strings in the whole universe, which was the last part of the Blood Shredder to be found, and Zoran was still just staring at it.

'We have all the three powers,' Dimitri spluttered.

'Mom will wake up from her longest sleep,' Theodore sobbed.

Dimitri put his arms around Theodore, who was kneeling down and just looking at the three powers that were the only way of bringing his mom, Isabel Blake, who sacrificed her life to protect Riffsland, back from her sleep. Theodore looked at Jonathan and Mendis. From his eyes, he was only trying to say that he will not be able to pay the debt for this help throughout his life. Finally the travelers of the journey were able to bring back the last hope.

They all came out of the jungle. The boat was still lying at the same place. Theodore was holding the String of Snakes, Pick of Dragon, and Buried Belt in his hand. He didn't want to let them go out of his hand for even a single second. The whisperer was sleeping on Mendis's shoulder and Mendis was raffling him slowly.

Everybody sat on the boat and Zoran pushed it. For the last time in their life, they looked towards the Island of Snakes, which was their last destination.

'What are you going to do after this journey?' Dimitri asked Jonathan.

'I will be going home,' Jonathan said.

'I don't think that The Three will have any problem if you will stay in Riffsland,' Dimitri said.

'I will talk to them about this,' Zoran said.

'I came here just to explore myself. I didn't know that so many emotions, lives, and faith will get attached to me. I am satisfied with what I have done and how I have contributed. Even if I will be going back with many unanswered questions, I will be happy forever that I helped a son in getting his mom back, a Nimbler in completing his debts left, a kingdom in getting its peace back, a lost shredder in getting his right place, and that's my achievement and reward,' Jonathan said.

'It will be really good if you will stay,' Zoran said glumly.

'I also want to stay, but my real world is outside Riffsland where my family is waiting for me. But we will meet soon, Zoran, and I will miss you a lot and especially when I will see a butterfly.' Jonathan chuckled and Zoran reacted in a way that he doesn't know what Jonathan was talking about.

'I will come to meet you in your world,' Zoran said.

'I will come to receive you,' Mendis said and smiled.

The boat was moving slowly in the ocean and everyone was looking towards the sun, which was going to hide in the mountains. The silence at that time was showing the upcoming peace in Riffland for which citizens of Riffsland were waiting for the past twenty years.

Jonathan with some unanswered questions, Mendis by proving his abilities and friendship, Dimitri by repaying some old debts, Zoran by helping in all of the critical situations when no one was left, and Theodore by completing the only aim in his life were now returning back to Riffsland where everybody was waiting with hope in their eyes and belief in their heart.